DEAD UPON ARRIVAL

A MADDIE SWALLOWS MYSTERY
BOOK 2

KAT BELLEMORE

KB PRESS

ALSO BY KAT BELLEMORE

A NOTE FROM THE AUTHOR

Before the Maddie Swallows mystery series came to be, I had written nearly two complete small town romance series. *Borrowing Amor* is my first and takes place in New Mexico. The second takes place in the small Californian coastal town of Starlight Ridge.

I love both.

But mystery has been calling my name for some time. I'm especially drawn to mysteries that have quirky characters and make me just as invested in their lives as I am in solving the crime. Books like Richard Osman's *The Thursday Murder Club*, and TV shows like *Psych* and *Monk*, come to mind.

When making the decision to start writing cozy mystery, I knew I wouldn't be leaving romance entirely, and I also knew that I didn't want to leave my characters.

There is more to these towns and the people in them than first meets the eye.

Which is why you now get to experience these lovely towns from a completely different perspective. One that now includes murder and suspicion, in addition to light-hearted humor.

And the characters you knew and loved from the romance series? They are now side characters, helping my sleuth on her journey.

Dead Upon Arrival is the second book in the Maddie Swallows mystery series. I hope you enjoy reading it as much as I had writing it. Because in writing mystery, I have found where my heart is.

Important Note: Your favorite characters do NOT die. Just in case you were worried.

"You can't hold out forever," I said, crouching and looking Ava in the eyes. She held my gaze, unflinching. "I know you don't care if I'm late for work, but surely you care if Flash and Lilly are late for school. You like them."

Ava didn't budge. Typical.

Good thing I knew her weak spot. I stood and grabbed a can opener from the kitchen. As soon as I opened the tuna, Ava would run from where she'd been curled up on my car keys, and I'd finally be able to leave. Walking to my office downtown was no problem, but the kids' school was a different story.

That cat loved the power she wielded and was on a constant quest to make certain we lowly humans knew our place in the world.

And it wasn't even my cat. Ava belonged to my best

friend and roommate, Trish, who had left for work as I'd been scrambling around, attempting to get my teenagers out of bed and myself put together.

And then there were my keys.

I opened the tuna, set it down by the back door, then ran. If given the chance, Ava would take a swipe at me. I'd thought we'd started getting along better the past few months, but then I'd made the mistake of picking her up from the couch so I could sit down to watch a movie— without her permission. I had placed her on my lap and even given her a good scratch behind the ears, but the damage had been done. That was when Ava had reestablished who was boss around there.

As I gathered my purse and phone, Ava did as I knew she would, running for the tuna. But she went out of her way to whip me with her tail as she went. That was fine by me as I grabbed my keys.

Look who had the last laugh now.

"Mom, I can't find my other shoe," Flash yelled from his room.

I was already late. Already rushing around like I couldn't figure out which way was up and which was down. Before the divorce, I'd always felt like a single mom, my ex-husband, Cameron, being in his own little academic world. We'd both been professors at the same university, but somehow, I had been expected to be more. Cameron had treated the parenting thing as a part-time gig that he took up when it was convenient, second to his career aspirations, which had left the rest of the responsibilities to me.

I had been wrong. I hadn't known what it was like to be a single mom.

Apparently, what little Cameron had done when we were married had actually been helpful.

Now, I was back in my small hometown of Amor, my two teenagers finally starting to adapt to the slower lifestyle (if you counted solving a murder earlier in the year as slow).

And yet life hadn't slowed down for me at all. In fact, it felt as if it had sped up. While Cameron was off doing book signings for his *New York Times* bestselling book, *How I was Seduced by a Serial Killer*, I was the one running around, making sure people had been fed, that they made it to school, and that my shirt wasn't on backwards. Yes, a client had had to point it out to me the previous week in our therapy session.

I glanced down, just to make sure. Nope, all good.

"Have you tried under the pile of dirty clothes by your dresser?" I called up the stairs. The pile that had somehow formed right next to my son's hamper rather than in it.

A pause.

"Nope, not there."

"Look in your closet. On the shoe rack."

Another pause.

"It's there. How did you know?" Flash sounded genuinely surprised.

"Because when I was cleaning last night, I put them back where they belonged, and it's the last place you'd ever look."

I heard a chuckle from the direction of the kitchen table. My mom had stopped by to drop off fresh pomegranates she'd picked from her tree that morning. When she'd discovered my predicament, rather than offering to help, she'd sat herself at the table and watched in amusement.

"Trish already gone?" she asked.

Trish had moved down to Amor with me when she'd quit her job at the same time I had. She'd offered to be my roommate to help out and save on rent, and I'd offered her the opportunity of opening Amor Therapeutic Services with me. She was a godsend, but she also couldn't be in three places at once, which was what was expected of me this morning.

"She ran over to open the office while I get the kids to school," I said. "They have a late-start day, something about teacher appreciation, so it's a bit more chaotic than usual. You could help, you know."

I grabbed an apple from a basket on the counter. It wasn't much, but it was all I was going to get until my lunch break. If I got one, that was. Everyone talked about how freeing owning your own business was, but that was only because they'd never actually done it.

Sure, I didn't need pre-approval to take off for a week and could go on vacation any time I wanted, but I also wouldn't have any money coming in. Either Trish and I worked or we didn't get paid. Sometimes I missed the guaranteed paycheck.

"You're right," my mom said, struggling to stand. I'd noticed her knee had been acting up again, and it seemed to be getting worse. "Let me make sure Lilly is up and that she's ready. You have a business to run, and those kids aren't pulling their weight." Her voice wobbled with pain, and it caught me off guard. I'd never thought my mom would grow old—she was an unstoppable force that sucked in everyone around her. But seeing her now— sometime while I had been away, she'd gone gray. She'd slowed down. And because of our tumultuous relation- ship, I hadn't visited. Had never noticed.

Things didn't have to continue that way, though.

We'd begun to mend our fences and, even though she'd never admit it, she shouldn't be the one climbing the stairs to make sure Lilly had actually gotten out of bed when I'd asked her to. I wasn't going to be responsible for making her knee worse.

"Mom, you take it easy. I'll go check on her."

She scowled. "I've seen that look. The one where you think I can't hold my own anymore. It couldn't be further from the truth."

I raised a pointed eyebrow. "You really want to be the one climbing that staircase? Go ahead. I was saving you from having to deal with an ornery teenage girl who is on her period."

That did the trick. My mom's lips clamped shut as she threw a wary glance up the stairs.

"I suppose I should let you take care of this one. I've been there, done that, and you could use the practice," she told me. "Besides, I should be getting home. Want me to drop off the kids on my way?"

I worked to hold in a laugh. Same old mom, but as I'd aged, her antics had become more humorous than infuriating. Although they definitely still had their moments.

"That would be great, Mom. Thank you." I turned to run up the stairs but was met with the welcome sight of both of my children descending. Flash's nose was buried in his phone, and Lilly was readjusting her backpack. I couldn't believe how old she looked. She'd be seventeen next week. Gosh, could I really have a daughter who was only a couple of years from graduating high school? I suddenly felt ancient.

I shoved down the feeling that I'd somehow missed out on my kids' most important years and nodded toward my mom. "Grandma will take you to school so I can hurry over to the office. You two good to go?"

Flash nodded without taking his eyes off the phone in front of him. "Yeah. Don't forget I have my competition this afternoon. Might not come down for dinner."

Which meant that he definitely wouldn't. "Where's this one based out of?"

Flash finally slipped his phone into his pocket and glanced my way as he passed. "London. Only five hundred pounds for the winner, but every competition gives me a challenge and a new way to improve."

That was my little hacker. Flash claimed he never did it without permission, except in emergencies. That he was training himself to be able to help people. Like when there had been a murder in town earlier in the year, and he'd felt like he'd needed to do his part to help find the culprit. I didn't like it, but I had to admit that his skills had come in handy.

And it had allowed Flash to be the only fourteen-year-old I knew that had fifty-thousand dollars saved up in the bank. Whether he ended up going the college route like I had didn't really matter—that kid was so gifted, it was scary.

"Say hi to Trish for me," my mom said as she herded the kids out.

I was uncertain if she'd meant that sarcastically, considering her feelings toward my best friend, but I acted as if it was genuine. "Will do. Thanks again, Mom."

I glanced at my phone as I walked outside. Looked like I would still need to drive after all if I was going to be on time for my first client of the day.

Ava ran past me and out the door in a streak of fur, giving my leg a whack as she went, as if letting me know she hadn't forgotten how I'd tricked her into giving back my keys.

"That's fine," I called after her. "But no one will be

home to let you in until this afternoon, so I hope you don't mind a little sunbathing."

Ava stuck her tail up at me and continued on her way, letting me know she really didn't mind. There was plenty of adventure that lay ahead of her.

I LEANED back in my office chair and closed my eyes. Rushed mornings always made me feel like I was forgetting something, and I hadn't had a chance to catch my breath since arriving at the office several hours earlier.

The brief moment of silence between clients was abruptly interrupted when the door burst open, and I sat up straight, my heart hammering in my chest.

Ruby, Mayor Freedman's younger sister, stood in the doorway, her eyes wide and panicked. She was normally quiet and withdrawn, especially since her husband had been killed in an airplane crash several years earlier. She hadn't left Amor since that day, too scared to use any form of transportation other than the bike she took everywhere.

It had taken months of prodding to get her to come in and talk to me, and then she'd rescheduled every appointment since. I'd honestly doubted I'd ever see her again, in a therapeutic capacity, anyway.

Something must have happened, though—something bad, considering how frantic she seemed.

"Hi, Ruby. I wasn't expecting to see you until your appointment next Thursday." And in fact, I hadn't expected to see her even then. For someone with a tragic background like Ruby's, it wasn't unusual to need to try therapy several times before finally being able to commit to it. It was difficult work, facing the demons of one's past. "If you'd like to get in sooner, I can have Clarisse squeeze you in tomorrow."

I tried not to glance at my phone, but I knew my next client would arrive any moment.

"I did what you asked," Ruby said, breathless. She collapsed into the chair across from me. "You asked me to do something different every day. Something small that broke my usual routine. But now there's this man. And he's invited me on a road trip to the hot air balloon festival. I said no, of course. I mean, me, in a car? Traveling across state to see people go up in a balloon of fire and air? It's an accident waiting to happen. But then I hosted Katie's baby shower this afternoon, and something snapped. I couldn't do it anymore. Everyone is living their life except me. I love Katie, I do. I'm so grateful she came into my brother's life. But if someone like her—someone who had lived a life that was filled with crime and deceit—if someone like that can change and have their happily ever after, shouldn't I be allowed one too?"

I stared, trying to gather my thoughts. "When I asked you to do something different, I meant go a different route to work, or change your brand of shampoo. This is big, Ruby. Awesome, but big. This man... Where did you meet him?"

I prayed I hadn't unwittingly thrown Ruby into the arms of an online predator, out to take advantage of grieving widows. We'd only had one session—I couldn't have done that much damage already, right?

"It was when I was picking up the cake for Katie's baby shower. I went to high school with the guy but hadn't seen him for years. You actually know him...Parker Loveland."

"Wasn't he the one you stood up on a date your senior year?"

Ruby's cheeks reddened. "It was an accident," she mumbled. Her gaze dropped, and I knew better than to push it.

Clarisse poked her head in, her expression registering surprise at seeing Ruby there. Ruby must have snuck past while the receptionist was helping someone else. "Your next appointment is here," she said.

"Give me five minutes."

She nodded and retreated through the doorway.

I turned back to Ruby and stood. "I'm happy for you—I really am. Talk with Clarisse on your way out, and let's get you scheduled so we can talk longer."

Ruby didn't move. "I need to go to the balloon festival," she said. "But I'm afraid. What if I have a panic attack while I'm there? I need someone there to help talk me down. Someone that will help me through it. I can't give Parker that job—he's the source of most of my anxiety."

"You can call me anytime, you know that."

Ruby gave her head a vigorous shake. "No. I need you there. With me. In person. Please, as a friend?"

This was why I'd made an arrangement with Trish that she would work with anyone I'd grown up with, and I'd work with everyone else. Counseling people I knew—it became complicated. The only reason I'd met with Ruby in the first place was as a personal favor to her brother, Sam.

"I don't know, Ruby…"

"Bring the kids," she pressed. "They'd love it. It wouldn't be like you'd be hanging out with Parker and me. Just enjoying some family time, and if things got rough, I'd have a safe place to go—a safe person to be with."

Personally, I didn't think Ruby was ready for this. I always advised baby steps, and this was the equivalent of leaping off a cliff. But she looked determined, her lips pressed into a firm line.

"Our family could use a vacation," I said slowly. "When is the hot air balloon festival?"

Ruby smiled, knowing she'd worn me down. "This weekend. We leave tomorrow."

2

I stood in line at the diner, watching families and couples eating together. The kids were waiting back at the house for me, all packed up and ready to go. We couldn't very well start this road trip hungry, though, and I hated cooking the morning of a vacation.

The man at the front of the line finished rattling off his order and then found himself a table. Just three more people to go.

I couldn't believe I was doing this—driving several hours north because a client wanted me there for her getaway weekend. Just in case.

You aren't doing this for a client, I told myself. *Ruby is my friend.*

Friend or not, I hadn't been able to drop everything to race up to the festival the previous day. My Friday schedule was always booked, and the kids still had school. They'd said they didn't mind missing, of course, but I couldn't just cancel all my appointments.

Ruby hadn't been ecstatic to hear this news when she'd called from the motel that she and Parker were apparently sharing a room at—something neither of them had planned on—asking me to pick her up for an emergency therapy session. She no longer felt prepared for a weekend away with a man she didn't know all that well, even if they had gone to high school together.

Telling Ruby that we'd be up there Saturday hadn't seemed to do much to calm her, but there hadn't been much she could do about it.

Melinda broke through my thoughts, snapping her fingers in my direction. "You okay there, Maddie?"

I doubted Melinda was asking out of concern but more so she could get the line moving. It had somehow disappeared, and I was now at the front of it.

"Um, yeah." I walked forward to the counter. "We need something easy for the road. Maybe four scones...make that seven. No, eight."

That earned a frustrated sigh from Melinda as she scribbled out what she had written.

Melinda and I had never gotten along very well, and I tended to steer clear when I could, but then again, no one seemed to get along with her. It was a miracle the diner did as well as it did, considering her surly customer service and mediocre food. The one person who seemed to be able to stand her company for more than five minutes was a new guy in town, Daniel. Of course, rumor had it that he was in the business of creating fake IDs, so there was that.

"I better add in something that has some nutritional value," I said, risking Melinda's wrath for taking far too long. I looked over the menu that had been taped to the counter. "Let's do three yogurt parfaits. Nope. Four. You never know if Flash will decide that he actually enjoys healthy food once in a while."

Melinda waited, pencil in hand but not actually writing anything down. "That it?"

One more scan of the menu told me that everything else would be far too messy to eat in the car, and I didn't want my seats smelling like egg for the next few months.

"Yup, that's it. I'll take it to go, please."

My phone chimed with a new text message.

Mom, when are you going to be home?

Lilly is forcing the cat to do a photo shoot.

She's threatened that I'm next. Please hurry!

I laughed as I gathered up the bags of food and hurried home.

What was a mom for if not to rescue her teenage son from an unwanted photo session at the hands of his sister?

"YOU HAVE everything you'll need for the weekend?" I asked the kids, shoving in the last of what we could fit into the back of our small car.

Flash slid into the seat and immediately pulled out his

phone. "It's not like we need much. Does the hotel have a pool? I packed a swimsuit, just in case. No hotel is worth staying at if it doesn't have a pool."

Lilly sat herself at the opposite end of the seat, attempting to put as much space as she could between her and her brother. I'd had high hopes for them getting along better as we settled into our new small-town life, but it seemed the only time they got along was when they were investigating a homicide, or when they were teamed up against me for a common goal.

"I have my good camera, and that's all I really need," Lilly said. Because of her academic struggles due to her dyslexia, she relied on her creativity to make her mark, and she was very good at what she did. Aside from her video diary that only she was allowed access to, she'd taken up photography and film since we'd moved to Amor. She had hopes of directing her own documentaries one day. "I bet the still shots I get from the festival will sell well at the farmer's market."

If the success of her previous photos was anything to go by, then yes, she would do very well.

"All right, if you're sure your camera is all you need," I said, hiding a smile and knowing she had a fully packed suitcase in the back.

I'd been subjected to Lilly's reactions when we dared enter her room before she was ready to meet the day, and I knew for a fact that her camera was not the only thing she needed to make this a successful weekend.

"Wait for me," my mom called from where she'd parked in front of my house. She lugged a large suitcase behind her, and I took a long, deep breath before turning to face her.

"Really, do you think the mountains is the best place for you to be going right now with that knee of yours?"

"You're acting like I'm old or something," she said with a frown, pausing to catch her breath and using her suitcase as a cane. "Unless you're planning on making me hike the whole way. Is that what this is—a backpacking trip where you expect me to lug all your stuff on my back?" She shot me a suspicious glance, like that really was my plan.

I shook my head. "You're sixty-five, Mom. You really think I would expect you to lug all our stuff? Of course not. I'll take half."

My mom hadn't been expecting that, and a cannon-like laugh burst from her. "There she is. My little Maddie has decided to return. About time too. I thought you'd left your sense of humor back at that university of yours. Either that or your ex-husband had stolen it."

My smile faltered, and I threw an anxious glance toward the car. "Not so loud, Mom. I don't speak badly about Cameron in front of the kids."

I hurried forward and took her suitcase from her. It was heavier than all of ours put together and had no wheels. Where on earth was I going to put this in the car? We had no room. "Mom, what did you pack? We're only going to be gone a couple of nights."

"Just the essentials," she said, and began counting off items on her fingers. "Blow dryer, curling iron, clothes iron, seven sets of clothes so I'll be ready for any type of weather, four sets of shoes for the same purpose—"

I held up a hand, sorry I asked. "Okay, okay, I get it. Preparation has always been your thing. I don't know why I expected anything less." It took some rearranging in the back and moving one of our smaller bags to the back seat, where it sat between Flash and Lilly—not a bad thing, considering how they'd been at each other's throats lately —but we got my mom's suitcase in and ready to go.

"We need to get going," my mom said, looking at her watch. "You took so long, we aren't going to get there until late afternoon. We'll miss most of the first day."

Breakfast aside, the biggest reason we were getting off late was because she'd called, asking for specifics about where the event was taking place, how long it would take to get there, where we would be staying, etc. And then packed a fifty-pound suitcase I'd had to finagle into my little car.

I had answered her questions patiently: Northern New Mexico, east of Santa Fe, it would take three hours, and we'd be staying in a hotel (though which one, I hadn't a clue, because I figured we'd just stop at the first one we came across in town). But now my patience was wearing thin.

"Mom, why did you invite yourself along if you were just going to worry the whole time?"

She paused as she was preparing to lower herself into the passenger seat, looking stunned. "I didn't invite myself. You asked if I wanted to join you. I'm coming along as a favor."

She certainly had a way of twisting words. This trip was supposed to be me, the kids, and Trish. But then my mom had caught wind of the impromptu road trip up to the balloon festival and had told Trish this was a family thing and that she should stay back and take care of the cat. Never mind that there were plenty of kids in town who would love to earn a little extra money by checking in on Ava while we were gone.

That hadn't gone over well with Trish.

Trish now stood now in the doorway, arms folded across her chest. She and my mom had never gotten along —I was pretty sure my mom was jealous of the time I spent with my friend, rather than her—and even when I'd asked Trish to meet us up there, she'd refused.

If it wasn't the kids fighting, it was my mom and my best friend. And I was getting a bit tired of playing referee.

FOUR AND A HALF LONG hours later, thanks to remarkably small bladders that apparently ran in the family, trees towered over us. One moment we had been surrounded by cactus, and the next by pine trees that seemed to come out of nowhere. Living in the desert, I sometimes forgot what it was like being surrounded by green. And as much as I loved the Southwest, a bit of mountain air always did me good. The road wound through the trees, up and over hills, but I didn't see any indication of a hotel and kept driving.

"Where are we staying again?" my mom asked, craning her neck to see out the window better. The sun was just beginning to sink, and I hoped we'd find someplace soon.

"Should be just up ahead," I said, praying that was true.

Signs advertising the balloon festival were plentiful, but any other signs of civilization were not. Then, just as I was losing hope, a building emerged. The motel wasn't what I'd been hoping for—seemed kind of run down. A truck was just leaving, racing out of the parking lot and skidding on the dirt as it went.

"Here we are," I said, fake cheerfulness oozing from the words. I pulled into the lot and parked in front of the office.

"You're kidding," Lilly said from the back seat, finally removing the earbuds she'd worn for the entire trip. "We are not staying here."

I looked at the peeling paint and the empty swimming pool next to the building. "What's wrong with it?"

Maybe if we kept driving, we'd be able to find something else, but it was getting dark. Besides, it sat on top of a hill and had a fantastic view, and it would be even better once the sun was up.

Flash got out of the car. "You mean besides the dead bodies that have been shoved under the beds?"

"It's not that bad," I said with a nervous laugh.

Yeah, it was that bad. And I was pretty sure Flash was right about the dead bodies.

"Mom, there's no way we can stay here," Lilly said, panic lacing her words.

My mom had yet to get out of the car. "You didn't reserve a room ahead, did you?" she asked, her tone accusatory. "That's just like you, Maddie. Always assuming we'll figure it out when we get there. But if you hadn't noticed, this is the biggest hot air balloon festival in the state, and rooms have been booked out for months. And if you think you can manage a campsite, forget it. Those are gone too."

I didn't bother to ask how my mom knew all this, already knowing she'd begun researching the moment she'd found out about the trip that the kids and I were planning.

"Relax, Mom. I got this."

I didn't have this. Not in the slightest. But I walked with what I hoped was a confident air through the door to the office. No one was at the desk, and there was no bell. I glanced around at the yellowed linoleum.

Yup, definitely dead bodies.

But we needed someplace to sleep.

Preferably two rooms so my mom couldn't spend all night telling me I should have checked accommodations before driving several hours on a whim.

Yes, maybe I should have checked. But I hadn't, and I wasn't going to suffer through my mom's reminder of it.

"Hello," I called.

Silence.

This place was definitely giving off Alfred Hitchcock vibes.

"I'm wondering if you have a room available," I called again.

This time, a woman appeared. A cigarette hung from her lips—I was pretty sure smoking wasn't allowed indoors —her tank top slipping off one shoulder. She didn't look like she cared whether I stayed in their motel or in my car, but she at least made the effort to look at her computer, which was a good start.

"We've been full for months," she said. "Should have made a reservation."

"I know," I said, uncomfortable under the woman's gaze. "But the thing is that I have a friend who is here at the festival, and she's never left our town before. Well, not in several years, anyway, and she really needed a support person, you know? Especially because she came up here with a man. Don't get me wrong, she knows the guy and everything. It's not that kind of 'going away,' but still, she needs me, just in case she has a panic attack. I'm a therapist, you know—"

The woman held up a hand. "I don't know. Nor do I care."

I struggled with my own issues of anxiety, and it

tended to make my mouth spew words like a runaway train. I clamped my lips shut. "You don't have anything?"

"We did have a gentleman check out early, but the room hasn't been cleaned."

Relief coursed through me. "Great. How long will that take?"

The woman shook her head, like she didn't know what she was going to do with me. "Housekeepers are gone for the day. They'll be back in the morning."

Oh.

"What if you just gave me clean linens and I changed the sheets and pillowcases myself? Maybe some cleaning spray, as well? And a vacuum."

The woman studied me before finally lifting a shoulder. "Probably doesn't need much. They only arrived yesterday and were gone for most of today. I can at least get you the linens, and housekeeping can do the rest tomorrow while you're at the festival."

She moved to grab the only set of keys that hung on a pegboard behind her.

"How did you know we're here for the festival?"

The woman gave a raspy laugh as she handed them to me. "Honey, everyone is here for the festival. You're late, though. If you hurry, you might be able to still catch the Balloon Glow."

I wanted to ask what the Balloon Glow was, but she'd already turned away. "I'll get you those linens.

3

"I'm just saying, we shouldn't have to make our own bed. Didn't even have gloves. Who knows what has touched those sheets? And did you know there would only be one bed? A king-size, sure. But for four of us, that doesn't really bode well, does it?"

I released a small sigh as I drove the dark, winding road toward the festival. This hadn't been the family trip I'd had in mind. "At least they had something. Better than pulling over on the side of the road."

But my mom was right, of course. Even for only two nights, this wasn't ideal. All thoughts of our predicament left when we drove over a ridge, however, and were met with the most breathtaking sight I'd ever seen. Hundreds of hot air balloons sat on the ground, lit up like Christmas trees. There were all colors and sizes, each one just as uniquely beautiful as the next.

"Oh my gosh," I heard Lilly whisper in the back seat. "That's incredible. I've never seen anything like it. Mom, pull over. I need to take a picture."

I obliged and could hear the clicks of Lilly's camera.

We sat there for longer than needed as I took in the view. Whatever else was going on didn't seem to matter in that moment.

"Mom, can we get closer?" Flash asked.

"Of course, honey." I pulled back onto the road, and we drove down the mountain switchbacks until we found a makeshift parking lot that had been created on the edge of a large clearing, though saying it was a clearing was an understatement. The balloons took up the entire area, nestled between the mountains, and all lighting up the sky.

Once parked, we were able to get out and walk amongst the balloons. The sounds of the burners as they kept the balloons afloat was deafening, but it seemed to add to the mystique rather than take away from it. Crew members held the baskets down so they didn't rise off the ground, and pilots kept the balloons just as filled as they needed to be to stay upright. They were handing out cards, which turned out to be trading cards that featured their balloon and its stats.

"I want a hot air balloon when I'm older," Flash declared. That should have struck fear into my heart, especially knowing that with his winnings from his hacking competitions, he could probably afford to buy one. But the fact that he might be interested in something other than computers and coding gave me hope.

"You'd need to find someone to teach you how to fly one," I told him. "From what I hear, it's a lot more difficult than you'd think. You have to know how to read the weather like it's your best friend, because you rely on it to safely travel. And when the weather is in a bad mood, you need to give it some space."

"Oh, so like Lilly."

I stifled a laugh as Lilly gasped in outrage.

"What about that guy," Flash said, pointing toward a particularly ornate balloon. "Maybe he'd teach me." It was blue and gold and in the shape of something like a genie's bottle. Beautiful swirls accented the balloon, and I was immediately drawn to it. When I looked to see what man Flash was referring to, it wasn't hard to pick him out. A man with cropped hair and a neatly trimmed goatee stood in the basket, waving at everyone as if he were in a parade.

I supposed he was in a parade of sorts, but this guy looked like he thought everyone had come to the Balloon Glow with the express intention of seeing him, as if he were famous or something. And maybe he was. But he didn't look like he knew the first thing about flying a hot air balloon. In fact, he had two other people in the basket with him. One man was doing all the work to keep the basket afloat, and the other was a woman who seemed just as enamored with herself as goatee man was.

Lilly snapped a picture of the balloon. "Ooh, I see a

balloon shaped like a chile pepper over there. A picture of that will sell out at the market for sure." She moved towards it, and Flash jogged to catch up.

"Make sure to take a picture of that ice cream sundae balloon on the way," he said. "Oh, look there's a s'more. And pizza. Aw, man, now I'm hungry."

Leave it to Flash to pick out any food-related balloons when there were so many others.

I hurried to catch up with the kids but stopped short when I noticed my mom far behind me. She didn't look so good.

"You okay?" I asked, jogging back. I glanced over my shoulder, making sure to take note of which direction the kids were moving in. There were so many people here, it would be easier to lose them in this crowd than at Disneyland.

My mom nodded but then shook her head. "My knee is acting up again. You go on. I'll catch up."

I felt guilty leaving her there, but also anxious not knowing where the kids were. "I can't just leave you, Mom. There's nowhere for you to sit."

"Sure there is," a man said from behind me.

I turned to find my childhood friend, Benji, standing there, grinning like a fool.

"What are you doing here?" I asked, wrapping him in a tight hug.

"I have a friend who flies hot air balloons, but I haven't been able to find him. Parker Loveland. You remember him? He was a few years younger than us. Anyway, while looking for him, I found a new friend." He nodded to a giant balloon shaped like a bucket of chicken. "His name's Arnold, and he'd love some company."

"Yes, I remember Parker Loveland." My thoughts jumped to Ruby and her weekend getaway. "He flies his own balloon?"

That wasn't good. I wondered if Ruby had known that when she'd agreed to come up here with him. It wasn't likely, considering her husband, Clark, had died in a plane accident.

I checked my phone to see if I'd had any missed calls or texts from her. No signal. Great.

I looked past Benji to a balloon that indeed looked like a takeout bucket of chicken. An older man, probably about my mom's age, stood in the basket, leaning against the edge with a slight smile, like he was taking it all in.

"Flash would love that balloon," I said.

"His crew consists of his two sons, who come out to the festivals with him," Benji said. "But they are busy keeping the basket down, so we got to talking, and it turns out he enjoys company. His wife died a couple of years ago; she used to be the one to go up in the balloon with him. Has a little bench in there even, for when he gets tired."

Benji gave me a meaningful look. Wait, was he trying to set my mom up with the chicken bucket man?

"Mom," I said, turning to her, but she was no longer there. After a few seconds of frantic scanning, I saw she'd already walked over and introduced herself to Arnold. He was inviting her in, and one of his sons stepped forward to help her up and over the side of the basket. It seemed it had taken no effort at all, his muscles so large, they threatened to break through his too-tight shirt.

And there was my mom, giggling away, like she was a teenager again.

"Huh. This is a weird turn to the evening," I said, my attention returning to Benji. I wasn't sure how I felt about my mom being set up with a random guy who flew a bucket of chicken as a hobby. Of course, I knew it had nothing to do with the balloon and everything to do with the thought of my mom dating. The woman had never gone on a date in my entire life, at least that I knew of.

And it shouldn't have made me feel weird, because the fact was that she'd been alone my entire life and she deserved happiness.

Benji's eyes danced with mischief. "You're welcome."

Speaking of dating.

My stomach flipped when I remembered how several months earlier, Benji had admitted that he'd had a crush on me when we'd been younger. No, he'd actually said he'd been in love with me. But that was before I'd moved away. Before I'd gotten my PhD. Been married. Been divorced.

I doubted he'd have fallen in love with the woman I'd become.

But still, there was that smile.

"I better find the kids," I said, trying to shake the unwanted thoughts. "If Flash has anything to say about it, they'll be close to one of the food-themed balloons."

"I'll join you," Benji said. "I need to find Parker's balloon anyway."

As we walked among the balloons, my breath was once again stolen from me. I couldn't believe how beautiful this was—how I'd always heard about the festival when we'd been living in Albuquerque but had never taken the time to come. I'd always been too busy. Too swamped with work. And I was only here because I'd been guilted into it by a client, and friend.

But the longer we looked for the kids, the less I was able to focus on the scenery, and the more anxious I became. I checked my phone—still no signal. "We're never going to find them with all these people," I muttered.

"We should probably get to a higher vantage point, then," Benji said, gently taking my arm and steering me to the left.

Floating above us was a balloon that was tethered to the ground with three strong ropes. Apparently, you could pay to have the experience of riding in a hot air balloon without actually going anywhere. And get a full view of the event.

"You're a genius," I told him. "Thank you."

But after waiting several minutes for the balloon to descend and the passengers to disembark, we were told there was a waiting list and it was full for the evening.

"Please," I said. "I can't find my kids. Could you take us up for just a few minutes...just long enough to find them? I'll pay you double your normal rate."

The ballooner hesitated, then nodded. "I'll take you up, but I'd be a crook to charge you anything for it. It's on the house."

Gratitude gripped me. I knew my kids were old enough to be on their own, but I still didn't like not knowing where they were and not being able to get ahold of them. "Thank you."

The man helped me in, but Benji vaulted over the side like a pro.

"Show off." I smiled and gently elbowed him.

But then came the realization that we were about to rise who knew how far off the ground.

"How high does this thing go?" I asked, trying not to betray how nervous heights made me.

The pilot tossed me an amused smile. "Tonight? Only about sixty feet."

Only.

I gripped the sides of the basket, waiting for a jolt when the balloon took off, but it never came. I was about to ask the pilot when he was going to take us up when I realized the lights of the other balloons were already falling away bellow us.

"We're already rising?" I asked, turning to him. "But I don't feel a thing. It doesn't even feel like we're moving."

"Smoothest ride I've ever had," Benji agreed.

The pilot laughed. "I get that a lot. It's even better when we're actually flying. We travel at the same speed as the wind, and it makes it feels like you're standing still." He nodded out to the balloon festival. "Is this an okay height to find your kids?"

I turned my attention to the mass of people below us. "Yeah, this is great. Thanks."

Being up there, above the lights and the people—it was distracting. Peaceful. I pulled out my phone to take a picture for Lilly. I knew it wouldn't compare to the shots she was getting, but she'd want to see it, nonetheless. She lived for moments like this.

"Will there be a Balloon Glow tomorrow night as well?" I asked the man. "My daughter would love this view."

"Sure. Tomorrow night, as well as the next."

I nodded, then resumed my search, trying to ignore how romantic it was up there—the darkness lit up by the balloons, the occasional sounds of burners going to help keep the balloons afloat. And how close Benji was standing to me.

Because he was my best friend. And I intended for it to stay that way.

"There they are," I said, spotting the kids by Arnold's bucket of chicken. They must have made a full circle and ended up back with my mom. My breath escaped with a whoosh of relief. "Thank you so much."

"My pleasure."

The pilot turned off the burner just as my gaze landed on the genie lamp from earlier.

"Is that one supposed to be rising as high as it is?" I asked, pointing to it. No longer were the crew keeping the balloon on the ground as it quickly rose into the air. The way people were scrambling below it, it didn't seem like its ascent was on purpose.

The pilot got quiet, and when I glanced at him, his skin seemed pale in the moonlight. "That man has no business being in a balloon, let alone flying one."

I gripped Benji's arm as I turned back just in time to see the goateed man who'd smiled and waved at us from his basket tumble out and fall toward the ground.

4

My knees buckled, and Benji's arm wrapped around me, supporting my weight. Holding on to the side of the balloon, I threw a panicked glance behind me. "Take us down, as fast as you can," I told him. "He fell right next to where my kids are."

It took a moment for my words to register, the pilot seeming to be in shock.

"Sir? We need to get down to the ground," I repeated.

The pilot snapped out of his daze and sprang into action, opening a valve and releasing the hot air, bringing us to a smooth landing. As soon as the balloon touched the ground, I leapt out and ran toward the chicken bucket. By the time I reached the kids, the paramedics were there, and security had established a perimeter, keeping people away from the genie lamp.

Thank goodness for that.

My kids were the type who would have wanted to get up close and personal with the poor fellow.

"Back up," a woman barked at some tourists who were trying to press their luck and get a look at the body. "If I catch you crossing that line again, I'm going to arrest you."

I knew that voice.

"Danielle," a man told her, "you can't arrest anyone. I know it's hard for you, but right now you're a security officer, not a sheriff."

I couldn't believe it. Sheriff Potts was here. The sheriff and I had a complicated relationship, but for whatever reason, in that moment, it made me feel better that she was there. I released a disbelieving laugh and turned to Benji. "What is Potts doing here?"

Benji scanned the crowd. "No idea. Sounds like she's in her element, though."

In her element. That was one way to put it.

The kids had moved from where they'd been standing and were now at the edge of the crowd, bobbing in and out, trying to get a better view of the accident site.

I rushed forward and pulled them into a hug. "You guys okay?" Surprisingly, they didn't fight it. "You didn't see anything, did you?"

Lilly shook her head. "No. We were talking to Grandma's new friend when we heard the screams. I like Arnold."

I hated that my children were in such close proximity to another death—there was no way the man could have survived a fall like that—but at least they'd been somewhere safe and not wandering around on their own. It had been less than a year since they'd snuck around, helping me solve a murder whether I liked it or not, and I really didn't want a repeat.

"Maybe we should call it a night," I said, turning to Arnold's balloon. He and my mom were leaning against the side of the basket, laughing. My mom looked happier than I'd seen her in a very long time, and I hated to break things up, but the less time we spent around the accident scene, the better. "Mom, time to head back to the motel," I called over, and ushered Lilly and Flash toward the car. "We'll come back in the morning when the balloons take off. I hear it's pretty spectacular." Maybe we'd be able to see Parker and Ruby with his balloon, now that I knew he had his own.

Ruby.

Oh, gosh. I hoped she hadn't seen the accident. That would be enough to send her into a downward spiral, and I wasn't sure she'd ever recover from seeing a man die on her first trip out of town. Especially given the nature of the accident.

Out of habit, I checked my phone. I didn't know why I had expected to suddenly have cell service. I'd have to call her from the motel room.

Lilly and Flash protested leaving so soon, not yet finished seeing the balloons. There were so many people at the festival, most of the pilots didn't seem to have any idea there had been an accident and were still handing out trading cards as if nothing was wrong.

My mom didn't seem to be in any hurry, either. As I drew closer, I realized Arnold was telling stories about the man who'd fallen from his balloon. He was so animated and had such a way with words, even Benji was listening intently, not quite ready to be done for the night.

They were humorous stories about a man who lived in a fantasy world and who treated everyone as if they lived on a lower plane than himself. Even if no one had liked the goateed man, otherwise known as Charles Reed—a name that wasn't nearly as exotic as the persona he'd seemed to have adopted—it didn't feel right to be telling stories of the deceased with him lying not a hundred yards away.

"Really, we're going to have an early morning, and it's nearly eleven o'clock."

Anything to leave. Why didn't I find this man's death as fascinating as everyone else?

My mom gave me an annoyed look, like I was intruding on her date, but before she had the chance to tell me as much, someone else called my name.

"Maddie Swallows, why am I not surprised to find you at the scene of yet another death?"

I knew I shouldn't find it funny—and a few months ago, I wouldn't have—but now? I couldn't help but laugh as I turned toward the sheriff of my hometown.

"Because trouble follows me, Sheriff. As do you, it seems. What brings you to the hot air balloon festival?"

Sheriff Potts liked to act tough, but under that hard exterior, she was one of the most insecure people I'd ever met. Everyone knew she hadn't asked to be assigned to Amor—it had been forced upon her. No one knew why, though. And whatever that reason was, it was the driving force behind her constant need to prove herself.

And yet, here she was, in a security guard uniform. The only thing that differentiated her from any of the others was her commitment to the job. The others looked like they'd rather be anywhere but here—like a dead body wasn't in the job description and they were rethinking their life decisions.

Sheriff Potts looked like she was going to go for her typical scowl but then didn't have the energy for it. Instead, she gave a resigned sigh. "Law enforcement doesn't exactly pay well, and I have a friend who was looking for additional security officers for the festival this weekend. Got my deputy keeping an eye on things in Amor. He was happy to do it—figured I could use the break. More like he'd rather not have me looking over his shoulder, making sure he doesn't mess up." She glanced back toward the deflated genie lamp. It now lay on the ground, and a photographer was taking pictures, the paramedics standing around, waiting for the body to be released. As I had suspected, the goateed man hadn't survived. "So much for my break," the sheriff said before doing a double take. "What are those kids of yours doing?"

At first glance, I'd thought the photographer taking

pictures was with the police—it was dark and difficult to see details in the scattered glow from the other balloons. It seemed the pilots had begun to realize what had happened, because even though the Balloon Glow wasn't supposed to end for another hour, they were already beginning to disassemble their balloons, creating odd shadows and dark patches across the clearing.

I took a step closer to the accident scene and realized the photographer was not with the police but was, in fact, my daughter. She'd somehow slipped past the police tape and was taking pictures of the balloon basket and whatever might still be in there.

When I hurried forward to get her out of there, a police officer stopped me. "Sorry, ma'am, can't let you past here."

"And yet, you let her in?" I asked, pointing to Lilly. If they wouldn't let me in, the least they could do was show her out.

To my horror, the moment the policeman glanced over to where Lilly stood, Flash popped out of the basket. Looked like my kids' sleuthing days weren't over.

I stifled a groan as the police officer hurried over, yelling at them to stop touching things. I turned away, not wanting to claim that they belonged to me.

Unfortunately, they ratted me out, and the officer hand-delivered Lilly and Flash to me, threatening to personally escort us from the premises.

"But don't you want to keep everyone here so you can question them?" Lilly asked, her tone innocent, but from her smile, I knew they'd discovered something that, as far as we knew, the police hadn't.

The officer snort-laughed, his stern exterior softening. "You've been watching too many crime dramas. When there's an accident, the witnesses give a statement, and that's about it. Can you imagine having to interview the thousands of people who are here?" He gave an exaggerated shudder.

"What about if it's a murder?" Flash asked.

Oh, no. We were not going down that path again.

"If it was a murder, then yes, it would be more extensive." The police officer glanced over his shoulder, like he was anxious to move on from this conversation. "Now, you two be good and enjoy the rest of the festival." He turned to leave.

Flash called after him, "Okay. Because it was murder. If you are interested."

The officer turned slowly back. "I'm sorry?"

"You really think a man who attends every festival with his balloon is going to accidentally fly too high during the Balloon Glow and then somehow fall out over the edge?" Flash asked, folding his arms over his chest. "Ask Arnold, over there in the chicken bucket. He'll tell you. This man, Charles Reed, was at every event across the country for the past fifteen years, despite not ever bothering to learn how to actually fly his balloon. He always had someone else do it. But the man has been all over the world. He's not just going to tumble out because he wasn't paying attention. The sides are much too high for that, anyway."

The police officer was breathing slowly, his eyes closed, like he was trying to control himself and not do something stupid. They were just kids, after all.

"I know that look," Sheriff Potts said, hurrying over. "I get it whenever I'm around the Swallows family." She'd apparently missed the conversation, because she looked between us all and then asked, "What have they done now?"

The officer opened his eyes and focused on the sheriff. "You know these kids?"

"I'm sheriff in their town."

Their town. Not *our* town. Sheriff Potts still wanted to keep as much emotional distance between her and Amor as possible. I tried to be offended by the insinuation, but I couldn't blame the woman. Amor wasn't the place you wanted to end up if you were attempting to have a prestigious career in law enforcement. No one would be singing her accolades, no matter how many criminals she caught.

Sheriff Potts was, and would always be, an outsider.

"They are attempting to tell us how to do our job, convinced that this was not a horrific accident but instead murder. All because they don't think the guy would fall out of the basket."

"He wouldn't," Lilly insisted, her pitch getting high. Uh, oh. It never went that high unless she was on the edge of a teenage freakout. "You think they didn't think of safety when they built these baskets? An unexpected thermal catches you off guard, you think they want people falling out of their balloons right and left?"

I hurried forward and placed an arm around Lilly, attempting to steer her away. Yelling at a cop, after tampering with his crime scene, was not going to end well. Lilly, however, didn't appear to be finished yet, and she threw off my arm and turned back to the cop. Before she managed to get herself into any more trouble, though, Sheriff Potts intervened.

"Actually, the kids do have a point." She turned to Lilly. "What were you taking pictures of?"

Lilly was so stunned that the sheriff was actually taking her seriously, rather than confiscating her camera like she'd threatened to do in the past, that it took her a minute to find her words.

"Just the crime scene—thought it might be good for clues later," she said. "I didn't notice any tampering with the basket. I had Flash pushing on it from the inside, but it held strong."

The sheriff nodded slowly. "Anything inside the basket?"

"Food. Lots of it," Flash said, his eyes lighting up. He patted his pocket, and I noticed how full it seemed.

Oh, gosh. He'd taken some of the dead man's snacks.

I prayed that no one else would notice and vowed to have an intervention with my children when this painfully long night finally came to a close.

"And wine," Lilly added. "Lots of that too."

Sheriff Potts turned to the police officer. "I know I don't have jurisdiction here, but I was hired to help with the event."

"The event. Not this investigation," the officer said.

Sheriff Potts couldn't quite stifle an eye roll, and I bit back a laugh. "Yes, I know. All I'm saying is that it wouldn't hurt to question anyone who was in the basket, as well as ground crew. See if anyone had a problem with this Charles Reed guy."

The officer grunted and strode off to talk to a woman who was sobbing next to the balloon. I recognized her as the one who had been in Charles Reed's balloon basket. The officer kept trying to ask questions, but whenever she tried to answer, she just ended up crying again.

"Please tell me I'm not that obnoxious," Sheriff Potts said, her attention on the police officer. When none of us answered, instead desperately searching for a new topic of conversation, her eyes narrowed. "I'm not, and you know it." And then she stalked off as my children snickered.

"It was like meeting a male version of the sheriff," Flash said, laughing. "A mirror image."

Yes, it was. We were used to only dealing with one of her, but now that there were more, I figured we should get out of there and back to the motel.

There was plenty of grumbling, not just from the kids but from my mom too. Benji had done a good job setting her up with Arnold—a little too good. But as we left, she promised Arnold she'd be back first thing in the morning to see him off. Of course, he then invited her to fly with him, and she nearly lost her mind, smiling so wide she looked twenty years younger.

It was nice seeing my mom happy.

But then we arrived back at the motel, and I saw I had seven panicked messages from Ruby, most of which were from that afternoon. Apparently, Parker had gone flying when he shouldn't have and gone missing for the better part of the day when his balloon crashed.

Of course he had.

As late as it was, I needed to call her back.

5

I listened to the rest of Ruby's messages and found the last one most interesting—the one where Ruby was freaking out because she had stolen Parker's car and driven back to Amor without him.

Huh. That was an unexpected twist.

It was well past midnight, but I doubted Ruby would be asleep. Not with the kind of day she'd had.

I stepped outside to make the call so I wouldn't keep the others awake. Not that I could sleep in the same bed as the other three, anyway. Once they'd all gotten settled, I'd known I'd be sleeping in the oversized chair in the corner. We'd need to figure out a better plan for the next day.

Ruby picked up on the second ring, wide awake, as expected.

And happy.

Not expected.

"Ruby, what on earth is going on? Are you okay?"

Ruby burst into the story of how they'd been staying at the same motel as us—and as it turned out, the same room. They were the ones who'd left abruptly, allowing us a place to stay for the night. She told me of all the fears she'd been able to overcome and how proud of herself she was, but that the weekend trip had ultimately ended with her being so furious with Parker that she'd left him and his crew and returned to Amor.

"I'm so sorry that I made you go all the way up there to the festival, and then I returned home," Ruby said. "I'll pay you for your trouble, I swear. And maybe you can still call me a few times a day when you have service, just to check in? I'm so conflicted. Parker and I had a long talk and—Maddie, I think I'm in love. That's why I left him today and returned home, you know. I'm in love with Parker, and it terrifies me. The man is a hot air balloon pilot. I mean, is that what I really want? I'll admit that it's probably safer than flying airplanes, but he was so reckless today. It's concerning. He received bad news from his parents and needed some space. I get it. If anyone understands needing alone time, it's me. But going up midday, and alone. After he crashed—I couldn't stand to even look at him. But people do stupid things when they are hurting. I can't fault him for that, can I?"

I rubbed a hand over my eyebrows. I loved Ruby, I did. But this was getting a bit out of hand.

"Ruby, I'd be happy to talk about things at your next appointment, but I'm with my family right now and—"

She interrupted me. "Hey, I have a call on the other line. Can you hold for a sec?"

And then Ruby disappeared.

It was the middle of the night. Who would she be getting a call from?

Ruby returned a few minutes later. "Scratch that. I need your help now. Why didn't you tell me there was a murder at the festival tonight?"

I blinked. "Someone died, yes. But the police are calling it an accident."

"Not anymore. Parker just told me they've canceled all events until further notice and that everyone needs to be questioned before leaving the event. I don't know how they expect to manage that. But they've taken Parker's crew member, Andy, in for questioning. And they're keeping him overnight. I haven't known Andy long, only since yesterday. But what we experienced in that short amount of time—we went on a rescue mission, Maddie. After Parker went up, Andy helped get him back. It's our turn to do the same for him. Will you go visit him, see if you can get him out of there?"

Looked like local law enforcement may have listened to Lilly and Flash more than the police officer had let on.

"If Andy is Parker's crew member, why would they think he had anything interesting to contribute? You guys weren't even here for the Balloon Glow."

Ruby was quiet for a moment. "I'm not sure. They said he was in the basket when the tethers were cut. That he was the pilot. But he's Parker's crew member—he shouldn't have been there with this other guy."

I pictured the genie lamp. The goateed man waving at everyone, like we were all there just to see him.

"Please," Ruby said. "Parker is beside himself with worry. So am I. Andy didn't do what they're saying. He's a sweetheart. A bit of a hothead, but a genuinely nice guy."

"All right," I said, giving in. "I'll stop by first thing tomorrow." With all the events canceled, it would give me something to do while we waited to be questioned.

What a fun weekend trip.

THE SMALL BUILDING that was supposed to pass for a police station sat along a barren strip of road, and I attempted to rub the sleep from my eyes as I pulled into the parking lot. That lumpy oversized chair in our motel room was not meant to be slept on.

"Wait in the car," I told my mom and the kids. Of course, they didn't listen to me, but I hadn't really expected them to.

Flash reached the station first, practically running in place, he was so excited. "I can't believe we're breaking someone out of jail. This is so cool."

"We are not breaking anyone out of jail," I said, keeping my voice low, just in case anyone was listening.

The last thing we needed was for someone to think that was what we were actually doing. "We are merely requesting that a man we have never met be released from police custody for a crime we have no idea if he's committed."

Yeah, it didn't sound so great when I put it like that.

"What's the young man's name again?" my mom asked.

I glanced at the motel notepad I'd written the name on. "Andrew Kern."

As we entered the station, I paused mid-step, blown back by the chaos. Dozens of people sat cramped in the tiny space, babies crying, children whining, as if begging to be freed.

I pushed my way through to a counter where a police officer sat behind a plexiglass window. He slid it open as I approached and asked, "You with the balloon festival?"

I nodded. "We arrived yesterday afternoon, but I'm not sure—"

The officer didn't wait for my explanation but merely handed me a clipboard. "I need your name, contact info, and the names of everyone in your party." He had a tired tone, like he'd already done this a hundred times. Judging by the full lobby, he probably had. "Did you witness the death?"

"Yes, though not up close. I was in a hot air balloon a ways away."

The officer released a long sigh, like this was news he could have done without. "When you are finished filling out the paperwork, please take a seat in the lobby until you are called back to give your statement. After that, you are free to go."

I hesitated. "All these people were witnesses to the accident?"

The officer nodded. "Yes, except it's a murder now, which is why all ticket holders were asked to immediately proceed to the station to give their information. All twenty-five hundred of you."

That must have been why we hadn't been contacted; Ruby had purchased our tickets as a thank you for coming up there to be with her.

"Is that normal procedure? To speak to every single person who was at the event?" I asked.

The officer's eyes narrowed slightly. "You're asking me if we're doing our job right?"

"N-no," I said, wondering how I could backtrack and make it sound better.

"You know that nothing happens out here except this festival, right?" he continued, his voice getting louder. "We do parking tickets. Not murders. We've asked for state police to come out, but instead they've told us that some small-town sheriff who was here at the time of the murder could handle it. Said she's former state police and could help out—that they are up to their elbows in other business, and they simply can't spare the manpower. Like we're not worth their time. Though we are free to send anything we'd like to their labs for testing. How kind of them."

"Oh, that's terrible." I tried to sound sympathetic, but the officer was still looking at me like I'd stolen his lunch.

Lilly grabbed my arm and pulled me back. "Way to make the police officer mad, Mom. Is your goal to get us thrown in jail with the guy we're supposed to be getting out?"

I ignored the question, because I didn't have a good way of answering it. Lilly was right, I was going to get us in trouble with my nosy questions. They'd probably think I'd done it and was sneaking around, trying to figure out what information the police had and if I needed to be worried.

There was nowhere to sit, so Flash let me use his back as a table while I filled out all the required information. My mom offered to turn the paperwork in, because she figured no one would dare arrest a harmless old woman.

I didn't know about harmless, but she did have a point.

It wasn't until after she'd half-skipped to the window, her bad knee hardly giving her any trouble, that I realized why she'd been so quick to volunteer. Arnold had entered at some point and was receiving his own paperwork.

A grin replaced his contemplative frown when my mom approached him, and he walked back with her to where my family was clustered, the paperwork clutched in one hand. "Got a strongly worded email," he told us. "Said we needed to give our information and be questioned in regards to the death that occurred last evening. I doubt they'd really track us all down, but I didn't want to give them an excuse. I'm continuing on to Zion National Park and the Grand Canyon after this. A tour of the best national parks that I've never been to."

"Sounds lovely," my mom said, hanging on his every word. "You know, we have a national park not far from us. Probably only a five-hour drive from here. White Sands National Park. It's breathtaking."

"You need a sled, but they sell some there," Flash said. "It's almost pointless going if you don't have one."

Arnold raised a questioning eyebrow but didn't get the chance to ask questions, because Sheriff Potts approached us at that point. "Looks like I'm staying a little longer than I was hoping, and in more of an official capacity. Turns out these people think they need my help, since I have some experience in this area."

She shared a look with me, most likely thinking of the recent murder in our small town of Amor. From the sounds of it, though, she had experience with much more than just our little place.

I held her gaze. "State police, huh?"

The sheriff stilled, and I swore I saw fear in her eyes. There was something in her past she really didn't want anyone to know about, and it seemed that it had started with the state police. Maybe she'd been a detective that had messed up. That would explain how she knew her way around a murder investigation.

"I'll be questioning you about what you saw last night," she said. "And then you will be returning home."

"But we just got here," Flash protested. "I didn't even

see a hot air balloon fly. They all just sat on the ground. I mean, it was awesome. But still, they can't just cancel an entire event."

Sheriff Potts turned to Flash, but instead of reprimanding him, she looked almost sympathetic. "I know it's not fair, and I'm sorry. But they can't hold an event where a man was murdered, without having caught the culprit."

"So, what you're saying is, if we caught the murderer fast enough, the festival could finish?"

The sheriff hesitated. I'd been caught in Flash's traps often enough that I knew exactly how she felt, wondering how the conversation had landed where it had and how to gracefully get out of it.

"I can't make any promises," she said slowly. "Even if we did catch the culprit today, many of the festival participants, and attendees, are leaving as soon as they can. No one wants to hang around with a killer on the loose. Especially when it doesn't seem like there's any good reason to stay."

"No promises," Lilly said with a sly smile. "But there is a chance."

She and Flash shared a look that struck fear into my heart.

Oh, no. They were hatching a plan to catch a murderer. Again.

"Oh, this sounds delightful," Arnold said. "May I join?"

"Of course you can," my mom told him, still looking completely enamored. "My daughter and her children are quite good at catching murderers. They solved Sheriff Potts' case for her just a few months ago. Didn't you, darling?"

Sheriff Potts gave me an exasperated look, like she regretted ever taking the weekend job.

"Of course not, Mom. The sheriff did a beautiful job in keeping our town safe." I turned to the sheriff, hoping she'd appreciated the sentiment. Because I now had a big favor to ask of her.

6

"Absolutely not. He's our prime suspect," Sheriff Potts said, folding her arms and leaning back in her chair. "Every one of our witnesses places him as the pilot in the balloon with our victim."

I paced across the makeshift office the local police had stuck us in, while my mom and the kids sat in chairs facing the sheriff.

"There was also a woman there with him," I pointed out.

"A woman who wasn't nearly strong enough to over-power a man of his size."

Very true. That was a problem. "Maybe our dear Mr. Reed was intoxicated. There was a lot of food and wine in that balloon basket."

"How do you know his name, let alone what was with him in the basket?" Sheriff Potts spluttered. "We never released that information." She paused in realization. "When your kids were taking pictures and walking all over our crime scene." She gave a quick shake of her head. "Never mind. Let's say you were right, and the woman was the one who pushed him over. Wouldn't that mean she had to be collaborating with the pilot? He wouldn't have just stood by while she murdered Mr. Reed. That means he'd still be involved."

Another good point. Darn it.

"What if he was intoxicated and fell over the side of the basket in his drunken stupor?" I knew I was grasping at straws at this point, and so did the sheriff by the incredulous look she gave me.

"Doubtful. Even if the toxicology report shows that he was drunk, your children were correct about the improbability of accidentally falling from a hot air balloon. The sides of the basket are far too high to simply take a tumble." The sheriff held my gaze as she said, "We are holding Andrew Kern." Her tone reminded me of my mother's when she was warning me not to ask again. "How do you know this guy, anyway? He's not from Amor."

"No, but we have a mutual friend. He's a crew member for Parker Loveland, a guy I went to high school with. Parker is dating Ruby Freedman, the mayor's sister. I think. I'm actually not sure what's happening there, but they traveled to the festival together. She asked for my help."

"Ruby was here with Parker Loveland?" The sheriff blew out a long breath. "That was some accident he had.

All of us were out there on ATVs trying to locate him." She rubbed her temples, like she felt a headache coming on. "Yesterday was not a good day for us. And it's not a good year for the festival."

"Please, Sheriff. Andy's a good guy," I said, trying one more time, knowing I didn't have a leg to stand on.

The sheriff actually chuckled, a rarity for her. "You don't know him."

No, I didn't. But we might know someone who did. "Talk to Benji. He can vouch for Andy. I know Benji is friends with Parker and has traveled to see him fly in various festivals. He'd probably have met Parker's crew at the same time."

"I can't let him go," Sheriff Potts repeated one more time, but now she seemed to be saying it more to herself than to us. She blinked a couple of times, as if clearing her thoughts, and pulled out a notepad. "I understand you saw Mr. Reed fall from his balloon."

And we were back to business.

"I was the only one, thank goodness."

My mom interjected, "That's not completely true, my dear."

I turned on her, panicked. "What do you mean, that's not true? You were in Arnold's balloon, and the kids claimed they hadn't seen anything."

"They didn't," my mom said. "But while they were listening to Arnold's stories, I got hungry. The only thing that man had in his basket was water, and I needed something of substance. The festival sold food there, you know, so I offered to buy some churros for everyone. I was just passing the genie lamp that this Mr. Reed owned, and that lady friend of his was yammering on about how many stars were out and how beautiful they were and stuff like that. Out of nowhere this crew member appeared and was running around the basket, as if there was something really important he had to do. Like maybe something was wrong, and he had to fix it."

Sheriff Potts was writing like mad now, pausing only to say, "Well? What happened then?"

"Oh, not much," my mom said, like the details didn't matter. "Although I do remember thinking how funny it was that he had cut the tethers like that, when I thought the whole point of the Balloon Glow was for people to meet the pilots, collect trading cards of the balloons, and all that. And why cut them? Shouldn't the young man have untied them? I mean, honestly, you're ruining your rope that way, aren't you? Wasteful is what it is."

I hadn't stopped to wonder why the balloon had been flying in the first place, considering that Benji and I had been flying in a balloon at the same time. Maybe the guy had wanted a view of the festival all lit up. Maybe he'd needed a breather from the crowds.

But my mom was now telling us that she had seen someone cut the ropes.

"Mom, why didn't you mention this earlier? You know, like when we were surrounded by police at the crime scene. They might have been able to catch the guy."

Sheriff Potts frowned and looked to my mom, like she'd had the same question.

But either my mom didn't notice or it didn't bother her, because she merely shrugged and said, "I don't know. Guess I didn't think it was important. Besides, I was distracted. I had promised everyone churros, and churros they would have."

More like she had been distracted by Arnold and her sudden need to impress the man. And apparently, she'd thought churros were the way to the man's heart.

Who knew? Maybe it was.

"Can you describe this crew member for me?" the sheriff asked.

My mom scrunched up her eyebrows like she was thinking, but I was pretty sure it was all for show. Rather than trying to conjure an image of the crew member, she was probably still thinking of Arnold, out there waiting in the lobby all by his lonesome. She'd hated to leave him there, but Sheriff Potts had insisted she talk to us individually.

"You know, I really can't say," my mom finally said. "It was dark, and everything happened so fast. I'm fairly certain it was a man, though. Tall. Yes, definitely tall." A pause. "I never did get those churros. Just my luck, the food stand had shut down just before I got there. Didn't they think people got hungry after ten-thirty?"

Sheriff Potts scribbled down a couple of additional lines, though most likely leaving out the part about the churros, then turned to me. "Do you have anything to add?"

"I'm afraid I'm not much help," I said, feeling helpless. "I saw the balloon rising and thought it was strange but figured it was tethered. And then I saw Mr. Reed fall. That was it."

Sheriff Potts didn't write anything down this time. Maybe my information wasn't useful. "You didn't see anyone push him or help him out of the balloon?"

I shook my head. "No. Just saw him fall. Wasn't even flailing. He just kind of...dropped."

It had been so shocking at the time that it hadn't really registered that I'd just witnessed a man's final moments. His death. It now struck me at full force, and my breath left me.

I had seen a man drop to his death. I tried not to imagine the terror he must have felt. No more waving at the crowds, smiling like he owned the world.

It had been over.

I wondered what his final thoughts had been—if he'd had any regrets.

I pushed the inner psychologist from my thoughts.

Because it didn't matter. What did matter was helping Parker's crewmate.

Sheriff Potts closed her notebook and slipped it back into her pocket. "Thank you. Your statements have been

the most useful so far. Everyone wants to think their information is important—the missing link. And sometimes it
is. But more times than not, people just want to feel like
they're the hero—they're the one who saved the day." She
paused. "I know you're just trying to do what you think is
right. But you really do need to stay out of this investigation."

"I promised Ruby I'd do everything I could to help her
friend," I said.

"And what if Andrew is guilty?"

I hadn't entertained the thought.

"Then you gotta do what you gotta do," I told the sheriff. "You won't find us standing in your way."

At this point, he really did look guilty, and I understood
why the sheriff would think so as well.

But I wasn't going to leave it alone until I knew they'd
done their due diligence—that they hadn't decided he was
guilty just because they didn't have anyone else.

"WELL, that was quite the morning, wasn't it?" my mom
said, strolling across the motel's parking lot like she didn't
have a care in the world. Her limp was all but gone, and
she lifted her face to the sun, smiling. "I do think we
should stay for a couple more days. You know, just in case.
I'd hate for Flash and Lilly to miss out on their first-ever
hot air balloon festival. I doubt they'd complain about

missing a few days of school. And we could celebrate Lilly's birthday up here on Tuesday."

I really didn't think the festival would be continuing any of the events, but I didn't voice my thoughts out loud, because right now the prospect of seeing the rest of the balloon festival was what was keeping my kids going. It gave them hope, and heaven knew we could use a bit of that in our lives.

And then there was Lilly's birthday. My oldest was turning seventeen.

"What do you think, Lilly?" I doubted she'd be thrilled with the idea. With the festival canceled, there was nothing to do up there, and she wouldn't have any of her friends. My mom probably just wanted more time with Arnold.

"Sure," Lilly said, lifting a shoulder, like she didn't care one way or the other. "Could be fun."

Okay, what was going on with her? No teenage girl would ever agree to spending their birthday in the middle of nowhere with no friends and spotty cell service.

Which raised another question: Why hadn't I heard one complaint about that?

"You sure?" I asked. "Maybe we could get back in time to have a party with your friends."

"No, it's okay. This Andy guy seems to need us more than I need a party. Besides, Grandma hasn't gotten herself kissed yet."

That was an image I needed to burn and bury.

My mom, on the other hand, seemed delighted by it. "Do you think he would? It's been so long for me, I wouldn't even know how."

I whispered in Lilly's ear, "Thank you for that." She rewarded me with a grin.

And time to change the direction of this conversation.

"Parking lot is pretty empty," I said, noticing that ours was one of only three cars there. "Either everyone is at the police station or..."

"They've left," my mom said. "Couldn't handle a little murder. Someone dies, and people run away like it's contagious." Her lips lifted into a mischievous smile. "But you know what that means?"

Before I could ask what was going on in that devious mind of hers, she'd already marched into the motel office and asked for an additional room, preferably one that was next door to where we were currently staying. "And make sure you clean it this time. Good."

I supposed their loss was our gain, and it certainly beat me having to sleep in that lumpy chair again.

"So...who gets the new room?" Lilly asked, looking like she wanted nothing more than to grab the new set of keys and finally get some alone time. But there was no way I was letting my kids have a room all by themselves while I—

"You two, of course," my mom said, handing the keys to Lilly.

My kids' eyes lit up and they took off, not bothering to

look back. They were probably worried that I'd step in and say no.

"Mom, we should have at least kept a key for ourselves. What if there's an emergency and we need to get into their room? If given the chance, they'd both sleep through a tsunami."

My mom simply adjusted her purse on her shoulder and walked to our room. "They need space—you smother them. If they require our assistance, they have phones. They'll call. Or knock on our door. You can do the same."

"I do not smother them," I muttered, having no choice but to follow her. There was nothing wrong with wanting to have family time or needing to know where they were, and who they were with. I'd always felt like I had to be both their parents, but that had only intensified since the divorce, considering their dad was now famous and mostly absent.

I didn't see how Cameron had enough time for his real job as department head at the university with all the publicity stuff he was involved with for his new book. The man traveled so much to speak at conferences and appear on TV shows, most of the time he spent with his kids nowadays was via video chat from one hotel room or another.

At least he made sure he always showed up for those. I supposed I should be grateful he still wanted to be a part of their lives.

"All I'm saying is that Lilly is going to be old enough to

be out on her own in the next couple of years," my mom said, opening our door. "You need to practice letting go. It will make things easier when the day comes." She paused before entering, and I nearly walked into her.

"She might not want to leave home right away," I said. "Maybe she'll want to hang out for a while. Help out at the therapy office. Or take online classes through the university." Even I didn't believe it, but I couldn't entertain any other possibility. I needed my kids. They were what kept me grounded—sane. Even as they drove me nuts, they were my everything. Who would I be once they left?

My mom didn't answer, though, and I saw her attention was directed elsewhere. I followed her gaze several doors down, where I saw Arnold entering his room.

"Oh, no," my mom whispered.

7

My mom ushered me into our room, closing the door quickly behind me.

"I don't understand what the problem is," I said. "I thought you liked Arnold."

"I do," my mom said, now pacing.

I'd never seen her look so worried—like she might throw up.

"He seems like a nice enough guy," I tried again.

My mom gave a vigorous nod. "Yes. Very nice. Too nice. It's fine when we're surrounded by hundreds of people. Fun, even. But this is different. His room is just three doors down from us. What if he sees that we're here? He's going to have full access to talk to me anytime he wants. All he needs to do is walk a few feet and knock on our door. I need distance, Maddie. Harmless flirting with no strings attached. But this... It's too intimate. I'm too available."

I held up a hand. "Let me get this straight. You've had no serious interest in this man and have been using him for your own entertainment?"

"Of course. What did you think was going on?" My mom gave me a look that said I should have known better. "He's just like your father, you know. Handsome. Smooth-talking. Charming in every way that counts. So of course I will be the one to leave before he can leave me. That's how it works with men like that."

A therapy session was the last thing I wanted to have with my mom while on vacation, but her views on men were so skewed that she was either going to spend the rest of her life alone or end up with someone who was awful for her because she didn't trust nice guys.

"Mom, just because Arnold treats you well doesn't mean he has ulterior motives." Before I could say more, my phone rang. I held up a finger, letting her know we weren't done with this conversation, and answered the phone. "Hello?"

"Maddie, it's Ruby. You had mentioned going over to the station this morning, and I know it's barely noon but just thought I'd check on how things went. Parker hasn't been able to talk to Andy at the police station, and he still hasn't been able to get ahold of his other crew member, Rafael. He's going out of his mind with worry."

"I'm sorry, but I didn't have any luck getting him released. I did the best I could, but Andy is their prime suspect."

"How could they possibly think that?" Ruby asked, her voice tinged with frustration. "I mean, what motive would he have had? What, he got bored and thought, 'Maybe I'll kill someone today? Never done that before, but thought I'd try something new?'"

I knew what Ruby meant, and none of this made sense, but it wasn't the motive that was our current problem—it was the opportunity. "He was piloting the balloon, Ruby. No one else was up there except Mr. Reed's girlfriend, and she couldn't have done it alone. The sides of the basket are too high for him to simply fall out."

"So, that's it? You're giving up?" Ruby's voice was rising in volume. I hated that I was the cause of her pain in the moment, but it was also good. She was forgetting her fears—putting the needs of others ahead of her own worries.

"I'm not giving up, Ruby. It's just going to take more time. We do know that there was an unidentified crew member who cut the ropes on Mr. Reed's balloon. I think there is more to the situation than what we're seeing, but there is still a lot we don't know."

Like how I'd managed to get myself into this mess. Murder. Again. I wasn't a suspect this time, though, and should have been on my way back home with my kids.

But it was difficult to say no to Ruby, who was the reason I was there in the first place. And to the kids, who so desperately wanted this thing solved so we could stay and enjoy the festival. Assuming there would be any balloons left by the time the murder was resolved.

I felt bad for Andy, I did. And for the victim, Charles Reed.

But we were talking about real malicious intent here. Someone had cut the ropes on the balloon, then thrown a man out of it. I really didn't want to put myself in those crosshairs.

Sheriff Potts was on the job—the police were in good hands. And if Andy was innocent, they would release him. I truly believed that, and not just because I was ready to go home and not leave again for a very long time.

Great, now I was sounding like Ruby, ready to put my head in the sand and pretend that would help all the bad things go away.

My mom must have been able to hear Ruby's side of the conversation, because she snatched the phone from my hand and said, "Ruby, it's Laurie Dawson here. You know, Maddie's mother."

I bit back a laugh. They'd lived in the same town together since Ruby was born—I was sure she knew who my mother was.

"The kids and I, we'd like to help you," my mom continued. I tried to take the phone back before she could make any promises she couldn't keep, but she kept it just out of my reach. "We are not going to leave this place until we have found justice for that poor man who died, as well as get your friend out of that filthy jail. I shudder to think what they feed those prisoners. A dangerous man is likely to be more dangerous if he's hungry, isn't he? I know how I get when I haven't had enough to eat—it makes murderers out of us all. Not that your friend is a murderer, of course—"

This time I did manage to snatch the phone from my mother's hand. "I'll keep you updated, Ruby. Take care." I wanted to leave the conversation on a positive note. "And I'm really proud of you. You've made a lot of progress these past few days. We'll talk more when I return to Amor." And then I hung up. Because if that conversation had been allowed to go any further, my mother would no doubt have promised that we'd show up on Ruby's doorstep, murderer in hand, to do with as she pleased.

My mother and the kids wanted to leave the motel immediately to go killer hunting, but I put a quick stop to that. It wasn't like we would even know where to start.

"The girlfriend," Lilly quickly said. She was stretched out on her queen-size bed, feet dangling off the edge. A bed of her very own. I tried not to be jealous. "It's always the girlfriend."

"She wasn't strong enough," Flash pointed out, not bothering to glance away from his computer that he'd set up on their room's corner desk. I had a feeling I didn't want to know what he was doing on that thing. Recently he'd gained a gray sense of right and wrong when it came to which websites he was allowed to hack into and which ones he wasn't. I, of course, had told him he wasn't allowed anywhere he had to sneak onto, but Flash had retorted that all criminals hid behind a wall of secrecy, and to catch the bad guys, some sneaking was required. He was just honing the necessary skills for a career in fighting crime, apparently.

"Could have been working with the crew member," Lilly said. "Maybe they were secretly in love and wanted Mr. Reed out of the picture. Maybe he wasn't as nice a guy as he seemed, and he'd hurt her if she ever tried leaving."

Flash snorted. "You watch too many of those dramas. Try watching a real movie for a change."

"Oh, you mean where everything is blowing up and the main guy just manages to make it out alive, all except his shirt? A few charcoal smudges being the extent of what he's had to endure?" Lilly sat up on the bed and smiled, like she knew she'd just won that argument. I had to say, I agreed.

"Surely the police are already covering that angle," my mom said. "If it's in a movie, they've thought of it. That's where they get most of their ideas, you know."

I smiled and shook my head. "Maybe we should let them take charge on this one, then. We've gone in for questioning—they have our information. Nothing they need us for now."

"But Andy needs us," Flash said, looking stunned that I'd think of not attempting to solve a murder case.

"You don't even know Andrew. Never met him in your life."

My phone rang, and I hesitated to answer it. It wasn't Ruby, though. Benji's face flashed across the screen.

"How are things coming on the case?" was his first question after I answered. Why did everyone think we were going to try to singlehandedly solve this murder?

"They're not," I said, making a decision. "Just need to get packed up, and we'll be heading back to Amor." I ignored the protests that erupted around me, from both my mother and my kids. What surprised me most, though, was Benji's protest.

"What about Andy?"

"If he's innocent, he'll be released."

A long sigh came from Benji's side of the conversation. "They aren't equipped to deal with something like this—they want it to be over. Not only from a law enforcement perspective, either. Right now, the festival is losing money, and they need to make it back. People are demanding refunds. The sooner they can get the festival back up and running, the sooner they can appease the public. Even for those who left early, they can't very well ask for their money back if the balloons are flying. And that means going with the most obvious of suspects."

He was right, I knew. But what did that have to do with us?

"Why are you so concerned about Andy?" I asked. "I didn't realize the two of you were such good friends."

"We're not, but I've gone out to see Parker fly quite a bit, which means meeting his crew, going out for steaks with them, that kind of thing." Benji paused. "He's a good guy, Maddie."

That was when the piece clicked into place. "Parker called you, didn't he? Ruby told him we hadn't managed to get Andy out of jail, and so he decided to check up on us through a different channel."

Benji gave an embarrassed chuckle, and it was completely endearing. "Kind of."

"If Parker is so interested in getting Andy out of trouble, why doesn't he drive back himself? And where's the other crew member you guys have mentioned? Why aren't they the ones going out and asking all the questions?"

A long pause on the other end.

"That's the thing," Benji said. "No one knows where Rafael is. He drove Parker back down to Amor because Ruby had taken Parker's car, but now no one can get ahold of him."

"But he drove down to Amor before the Balloon Glow?"

An exasperated sigh. "Rafael didn't kill Mr. Reed and then set Andy up. You're trying to find a setup where there is none."

It was true. Just like the police, I was trying for the most obvious suspects—the ones that were closest to latch onto.

Weird that no one had been able to find Parker's other crew member, though. It didn't make him guilty, of course. It was just...strange.

"Okay, no crew member. But what about Parker?"

"Forget about Parker. He's having some...family issues that he needs to take care of. He doesn't feel like he can leave them right now, and he's relying on us."

I wanted to mention, once again, that I didn't even know Parker, or Andy.

But then I noticed another call coming through.

Sheriff Potts.

Well, that was a surprise.

"Benji, I'm sorry, but it's not our place. I have a call on the other line, but we'll talk soon."

As soon as I answered, Sheriff Potts began speaking quickly, her tone hushed.

8

"The White Envelope," Sheriff Potts said. "That's the hotel where Charles Reed was staying. His girlfriend, Casey McKinnon, is still there. We've already spoken with her, but you might get something more useful."

My mind spun, and I tried to make sense of things. What was the sheriff doing calling me? Couldn't she lose her job for this? The woman was a formidable rule-follower, and I wasn't someone she liked enough to change that attribute for. "I'm sorry, the white...what?"

"The White Envelope. It's a play on words. You know, because the balloon part of the hot air balloon is called the..." Sheriff Potts released a sigh. "You know what, never mind. It was a mistake to call you. Stick around town for another couple of days, and we'll be in touch."

Someone must have been breathing down the sheriff's

neck for her to reach out in the first place, and I wondered who. I'd thought she was the one running the show now.

"I'm sorry, you just caught me by surprise. I'm all up to speed now. Except for the reason you want me to go out there at all. I thought you were handling this."

A hesitation. "I am. But these local guys don't know what they're doing. They don't like that I've been put in charge, and they're putting roadblock after roadblock in front of me. A lot is riding on me doing a good job on this, Maddie, and they aren't allowing me to do it."

I couldn't help but wonder if she'd received a call—a call that had threatened her with an extended sentence in our lovely town of Amor if she didn't wrap things up nicely. Or promised her a way out if she did. Either way, Sheriff Potts seemed more determined than she had the last time we'd spoken, but less secure in her abilities.

"So, you want me to do your job for you."

That had been the wrong thing to say.

"You know what, never mind," Sheriff Potts said, her voice rising in anger. "I thought you'd want to help an innocent guy get out of jail, especially when I understand that you have some personal reasons for doing so. Sorry for wasting your time."

And then she hung up.

I slowly lowered the phone and slipped it into my pocket.

"We're going to help the sheriff, right?" Lilly asked, her eyes lit up in excitement.

Flash's fingers flew over the keys on his laptop. "Of course we are. Mom can't ignore a plea from the sheriff. The sheriff needs us."

"How did you get all that from just your mom's side of the conversation?" my mom asked the kids, and I nearly laughed at how incredulous she sounded. As if she had perfect hearing, and it was only by some form of magic that my teenagers were able to overhear things she wasn't.

Lilly lifted a shoulder. "Easy. My mom said that Sheriff Potts wants us to do her job for her."

And then there was that.

I nearly told the kids no again. That was what responsible parents did. They didn't allow their children to participate in murder investigations. Except, and I knew every parent thought this of their own offspring, my kids were no ordinary teenagers.

And something the sheriff had said now played on repeat.

"She says that Andy is innocent," I murmured, more to myself than anyone else. "And it wasn't like she thought he might be innocent—she said it like she knew he was."

Flash and Lilly shared grins. "Does that mean we get to investigate?" Lilly asked. She said it like she already knew the answer.

I supposed it wouldn't hurt to poke around the White Envelope a bit. Hopefully it would be nicer than the place we were currently holed up in, with its abandoned swimming pool and peeling paint.

"No," I said slowly. "But I thought it might be nice to get outside for a while. Go for a drive. I hear there's a nice hotel just up the road. Maybe they'll have a restaurant or a pool we can visit."

Flash glanced up from his computer. "When you were on the phone with Sheriff Potts, you said, 'The white... what?'" He looked at his screen. "Only hotel around here that matches the description is the White Envelope. It's about fifteen minutes up the road. I'm assuming that's where we're going?"

So much for plausible deniability. I tried to keep things from my kids, and they still managed to steamroll ahead, a large neon sign announcing our arrival.

"Yes, that's where we're going. But could you keep it down about the investigation? We're not supposed to be snooping around, and the sheriff was definitely not supposed to feed us that information."

"Mum's the word," my mom said, miming zipping her lips, locking them, then throwing away the key. Flash pretended to catch it midair, then swallow it.

"To our first murder suspect," Flash yelled, then shut down his computer, swung the door open, and ran outside.

And that was how we kept things quiet in our family.

THE WHITE ENVELOPE was certainly a few stars nicer than the place we were staying at. It loomed above us, and a valet stood ready to park our car.

"Um...do you have self-parking?" As soon as I asked it, I could feel his judgment. Yes, I wanted to save myself some money, and no, I didn't want to have to tip the nice young man for something I could do myself. But they didn't have self-parking, and I handed my keys over.

I was annoyed at having to use the valet service, but that didn't compare to how I felt as soon as I'd exited the car and walked into the hotel's lobby with my family.

My mom turned in a circle, taking in the high ceilings and shiny columns that surrounded us. "I feel so..."

"Small," I finished for her.

Small. Inconsequential. Like I had made a wrong turn at some point in my life, and I had missed out on giving my family privilege...money.

My mom threw me a quizzical look. "No, honey. Not small. I feel pity. Sure, maybe none of us slept well last night because we were all squished together. But we were as close as any family can get. And I wouldn't have it any other way. This place—it's too big. Impersonal. Empty. Mr. Reed stayed in this place, and look at what happened. He's dead."

"I hardly think that happens to all their guests," I told her with an amused smile.

My mom huffed. "Maybe not. But I guarantee the reason he's dead is because of that money he enjoyed flashing around. Arnold told me all about the young man. Rich before he was born, and privileged. Couldn't even be bothered to fly his own hot air balloon—knew nothing about it except that he wanted it. There were always three people in that basket. Mr. Reed, a lady friend—always someone different—and the pilot."

Okay, so not a likable guy. But that had more to do with Mr. Reed than his money.

Of course, I'd never had much money to speak of, so who was I to judge? Maybe it had everything to do with his money.

"Shall we see if his current lady friend had something to gain?" I said, then approached the desk.

A woman stood behind it, and her eyes immediately scanned me, as if sensing whether I was a guest she needed to take special care of.

I wasn't, if her apparent disinterest was any indication.

"All of our rooms are full, and we don't know when we'll have another opening," she said, then returned to her current task.

"I doubt that your rooms are full—people can't get out of this town fast enough," my mom said. "Maybe the reason you aren't taking reservations is because one of your guests was murdered."

I hadn't even realized my mom had walked up beside me, and I wanted to smack my palm against my forehead. "Let me handle this," I said under my breath.

The woman behind the desk looked shocked but then quickly recovered. "There is an ongoing investigation, yes. But like I said, we are full. If you'll excuse me, I have work to do."

"Oh, well, we wouldn't want to disrupt your work," my mom continued, smiling and appearing to be a harmless older woman who didn't have a bone of deceit in her body. "If you'll just let us know what room we can find Ms. Casey McKinnon in, we'll be on our way."

That got the desk clerk's attention, and not in a good way.

"I'm sorry, who did you say you were?" she asked, her eyes narrowing.

I doubted she'd believe we were with law enforcement, unless it was bring-your-entire-family-to-work day.

Flash and Lilly hurried to my side and smiled at the lady. "Casey is our aunt, and she promised we could go swimming in your pool," Flash said. "We're only visiting for the day, and I know that it's horrible what happened to Uncle Charlie, but we were already nearly here when we heard the news. That's what we called him...Uncle Charlie. He wasn't really our uncle, of course, but we thought of him as one. He'd promised us a flight in his balloon, but since that isn't going to happen, Aunt Casey said we could go swimming instead. Not exactly the same thing, is it? My sister Lilly was pretty mad about the change of plans, but Aunt Casey says you can't predict when someone is going to tumble out of a hot air balloon, and you just have to deal with it sometimes."

I laid a hand on Flash's shoulder, desperately hoping he'd get the hint that he'd gone on long enough, and he was just as likely to get us in trouble as he was to help us.

The desk clerk looked pretty taken aback herself, like she wasn't sure what to make of the latest development, when a woman approached us. She was tall and lean, her blonde hair pulled back in a messy bun, and yet she still managed to look like she'd just walked off a magazine cover.

Casey McKinnon.

"If it isn't my favorite niece and nephew." She smiled widely as she studied Flash and Lilly, before her gaze landed on me. "You're early, sis, but no matter. How about we see to that swim I promised you?"

I stared. Casey knew how to lay it on even thicker than Flash. And that was saying something.

Flash, on the other hand, didn't miss a beat. He did a victory dance and yelled, "Awesome," in true teenage boy fashion. Then he turned and waved to the desk clerk. "Looks like Aunt Casey has everything taken care of, but if we need anything, you'll be the first person we call."

Said just like the rich and spoiled child that he wasn't. It was a good thing too. I shuddered to think what he'd be like if we had money for real.

I managed to recover from my surprise long enough to thank the desk clerk, then hurried after "Aunt Casey," who had grabbed a complimentary chocolate from a bowl on the desk, then turned on her heel and was already leading us away from the entryway.

"Now, do you want to tell me who you are?" Casey asked, her tone no longer welcoming. Instead, it was brisk and sharp, though she still wore a large smile. "You're not cops, and you're not reporters. That's the only reason I rescued you back there." She glanced back at my mom and me. "I don't know if you realized it, but you were three seconds away from hotel security escorting you outside. Or worse. They ran a tight ship before Charles's death, but it's nearly impenetrable now. I can guarantee we're being watched on the cameras right now."

Hence the smile.

I returned it to help keep up appearances and not give away that I was so nervous, my hands were shaking and I could barely keep my purse on my shoulder. "Your boyfriend was murdered, and our friend has been falsely accused. He was in the basket with you at the time of the death."

That gave Casey pause. "Andy. Yes, I told the police he couldn't have done it, but no one believed me. Well, except one woman, but the men made sure they put her in her place. Horrible how we're treated in male-dominated careers, isn't it?"

That must have been Sheriff Potts.

"Yes, terrible," I agreed. "Why do you say it couldn't have been him, if you don't mind me asking?"

Casey didn't respond right away, instead leading us outside and toward the most beautiful pool I'd ever seen. Palm trees towered above it, and the water was so clear, it sparkled.

"Because he was working like mad to bring us back

down. We hadn't realized the ropes had been cut, and no one was responding on the radio. He opened the flap to let some of the hot air out, but too much escaped at once, and we dropped rather suddenly."

"Was that when Mr. Reed fell from the balloon?"

Casey nodded, her gaze dropping. "I had stumbled against the side of the basket, and when I looked back to make sure Charles was okay, he was...gone." Her voice hitched on the last word, and she wiped at her eyes.

Well, this had just gotten interesting.

Because if my training in psychology had taught me anything, it was this.

Casey McKinnon was lying.

9

We hadn't gotten further than the edge of the pool when security appeared. A burly man in a too-tight polo materialized at my side. If he thought he blended in by dressing like a common employee, he'd never looked in the mirror. I'd never mistake him for a pool boy—not with muscles that were larger than my head.

"It's time for you to leave," he told us.

Flash immediately injected himself into the conversation, and I wished he hadn't. "But Aunt Casey invited us to come swimming with her."

The security guard raised an eyebrow. "Where's your swimming suit?"

Flash spluttered, apparently not having thought of that. And then, quick-witted boy that he was, he proudly puffed out his chest and said, "I swim in the nude." And then he proceeded to pull off his shirt and throw it to the ground. The rest of us gaped as Flash began on the top button of his pants—I had no desire to see how far he was going to take this—when the guard grabbed him by the arm.

"You can take your nudity elsewhere."

My mama bear kicked in, and I yanked Flash from the man's grasp and told him what I thought of his treatment of my son. It only took three minutes for the four of us to be standing on the pavement in front of the hotel, wondering how people got their cars back when they'd been taken by a valet. Especially when the valet was not there, and I didn't dare go back into the hotel to ask.

"At least Casey didn't get in trouble," Lilly said. "I don't think we could fit another person in our motel room."

Casey. Yes, she was a puzzle. The way she'd rescued us at the counter like that, but then lied about what had happened at the time of Mr. Reed's death. Almost like she'd been curious about our presence and how much we knew.

It had also been her who had called security on us. I wasn't sure how she'd done it, but right before the burly guard had grabbed Flash, I'd seen him exchange looks with Casey. She'd given a curt nod, then disappeared as the rest of us had been dragged away.

My mom had been quiet this whole time, and when I turned, I realized she was no longer with us. Before I had the chance to ask where she was, our car came peeling around the corner. "Get in," she yelled.

I was unsure if she'd just stolen the car, but considering it was ours to begin with, I didn't worry about it too much as we all piled in.

"The valet had all the keys hanging in a box right there," my mom said, nodding to a stand next to the valet's booth. "Now that I think about it, I should have taken all the keys. Then I could have had my pick of the litter."

I shook my head. "Mom, please, at least attempt to be a good example for my kids. Or pretend. But grand theft auto isn't how we do things in our family."

"I got your car back, didn't I?" my mom said, even as she peeled away from the hotel.

It was a miracle we all got back to the motel in one piece, but once we reached the parking lot, the kids had a good laugh about their grandma providing the getaway car. Even I couldn't help but join in. As we approached our rooms, I scanned the conspicuously empty lot and decided to take a detour. One that I would rather take on my own. "I'll meet you in our room in just a minute," I told my mom, then wandered over to the motel's office. Even if the clerk at the White Envelope wouldn't be any help, this was a small town, and if gossip was anything like in Amor, the clerk at our own motel would work just fine.

The same woman with a cigarette hanging from her lips sat behind the counter.

"Bunch of people check out?" I asked as I wandered in.

The woman was flipping through a magazine and didn't bother to look up. "Uh-huh."

I tried again. "Thought we were all supposed to stay put. You know, with investigations underway for that murder and everything."

The woman shrugged and turned a page. "Folks figured they'd already given the police their information, and they didn't want to stick around with a murderer loose. Can't say I blame them. No use keeping them here, anyway. Not like Chuck was staying in our motel. Too good for us now that he has loads of money."

Chuck. Short for Charles. "Mr. Reed didn't always have money..." I looked for a nametag. "...Valerie?"

Valerie snorted and finally looked up. "Chuck? Naw, he grew up in these parts and worked the festival just like the rest of us. He was a crew member for hire. Basically, if a balloon could use an extra hand, they hired him. Helped take care of his mama that way."

He knew his way around a balloon more than I'd been told. And I wondered how extensive that knowledge was.

"I suppose getting a balloon in the air is different than actually flying one, though," I said.

Valerie gave a slow nod. "True. But Chuck knew how to do it all—never wanted to be outdone."

"But then why did he always have a pilot up there with him?" This was more of an internal musing, but Valerie had an answer for that as well.

"Because he was a pompous jerk. He spent a lot of time

with the rich folks that would hire him as their crew, and then he started getting invitations to do things outside of balloon festivals. You know, socially. Before you know it, the man was dressing himself like he's the Count of Monte Cristo and buying his ridiculous genie's lamp balloon, hiring pilots so he doesn't have to do any work himself—I mean, the man was nothing but a mirage."

Well, this was a different picture than the one I'd been given.

"What about his girlfriend? Think she knows any of that?"

"Casey?" Valerie laughed. "No, she's just there because Chuck told everyone he was born into money. That woman is almost as fake as he was. Almost."

Huh.

I turned to leave, but then paused. "Valerie, do you have another room with two queen-size beds that my mom and I could switch to? Preferably one that is already clean? As much as I love my mother, I'd rather not share a bed with her." The largest bed in the world wouldn't be big enough to share with my mother.

Valerie nodded, seeming to have warmed up to me, thanks to our little gossip session. "Sure thing. Most of the people here didn't bother going to the police station, just hightailed it out of here. They'll regret it, of course—I was asked to give the names of everyone who was staying here over the past few days. Can't outrun our local law enforcement. They don't got nothin' else to do, and this is the most exciting thing that's happened in a long time." She clacked away on her computer, then removed a set of keys from the pegboard behind her.

"And most of your police officers probably knew Charles," I guessed.

"That they did, though I don't know that has anything to do with it. No one in town could stand Chuck, and we were okay with him only popping in once a year for the festival. Of course, he acted like we were all best friends, but we knew it was just him trying to flaunt his new life-style. Like he was gracing us with his presence or something." Valerie held out the key to me. "Got you the one next door, room 206."

I took it and gave her a grateful smile. "Appreciate it."

"How long do you think you'll be sticking around?" she asked. "Just so I know how long to reserve your room for. I can extend your other room too, if you need it."

I really didn't want to stay longer than necessary. The kids might be able to skip school, but I still had a therapy office and patients to see.

Even so, something wasn't sitting right with me about this whole situation, and I wondered how many people in town had had enough of Charles Reed's flaunting. Enough that they had somehow orchestrated for him to fall out of a hot air balloon.

"Let's start with two nights."

Valerie nodded and typed something into her computer.

While she was distracted, I nonchalantly leaned against the counter and asked, "Anyone hold a big enough grudge against Charles to want to kill him?"

Her fingers paused, and she glanced up, her eyebrows scrunched. "What is that to you?"

Guess we weren't good enough friends to ask something like that. I should have known, with this being a small town similar to my own. Maybe even smaller. They were happy to gossip, but I was still an outsider, and I wasn't to be trusted. Not when I was going around asking questions like that.

I raised a shoulder. "Just that if we're sticking around for a couple more days, I'd like to know if there's anyone I need to be careful around. I have kids, you know."

Valerie's features relaxed, and she turned back to her computer. "Oh, you don't have to worry about that. Whoever got Chuck, it was personal. It's not like we have some psycho running around town randomly pushing people out of hot air balloon baskets."

"He was that bad, huh?"

"Oh, sure. He had a reputation among the pilots. Not only did the guy not fly his own balloon, but he routinely stole girlfriends—wives. Just for the weekend, mind. Then he'd dump them and move on to the next festival. The man could spin lies like you wouldn't believe. Didn't care whose lives he destroyed as he flew through each new place. Every pilot knew to steer clear of him."

The way Valerie said it, it almost sounded like she knew from personal experience.

"I suppose it was nice having all that attention—something he must not have had before he had access to all his money."

Valerie stepped back from the desk. "Don't make excuses for Chuck. Whatever his past, he absolutely deserved the ending he got."

And then she disappeared into the back of the office without so much as a goodbye.

10

"I don't know why we have to change rooms," my mom grumbled as she folded one of her blouses. I walked over and helped place her things in her suitcase. She was the only person I knew who unpacked everything and actually used the dressers provided by the motel.

"I love you, Mom, but I need space when I sleep. I've gotten used to having my own bed."

My mom threw her brush into her bag and turned on me. "But this trip was supposed to bring us closer, and the first chance you get, you rush off and try to put as much space between us as you can."

I hadn't thought of it that way; I'd just wanted to get a good night's sleep.

"I'm sorry, Mom, I didn't mean to hurt your feelings. If it makes you feel better, I just talked with Valerie, the desk clerk, and our victim, Charles Reed, wasn't as he seemed.

Turns out that he's originally from here, didn't have any money to his name growing up, and apparently no one liked him. He was vain and thought everything was his, including the other pilots' wives."

"How is that supposed to make me feel better?" my mom snapped. It was true, one had nothing to do with the other, but then her lips twitched up into a small smile. "Okay, it did help a little. Looks like we have a full-fledged mystery on our hands. The man who pretends he is someone he's not and who has given an entire town motive to kill him. Not to mention the hot air balloon community."

When she put it that way, I felt much worse about things. Like I wanted to run away and let the professionals take care of this, even if it meant my kids not being able to see the remainder of the festival.

Even if it means Andy staying in jail?

The thought nagged at me, and I thought of Ruby, begging for my help. I released a sigh.

"We need to find someone who can give us more insight into Charles Reed—the real Charles Reed—and who might have killed him." I threw a glance at my mom. "Once we change rooms, we're visiting your new friend, Arnold."

My mom's eyes widened. "Oh no we're not. He can't know we are in the same motel. You can't make me."

. . .

AND THEN THERE WE WERE, standing in front of Arnold's motel door, my mom shifting her weight from foot to foot, like she was ready to make a run for it.

"Thanks, Mom. I owe you one," I said, my voice soft.

"You bet you do. In fact, as soon as this murder is solved, you owe me three or four. A mystery, I like. But this—"

The door swung open.

My mom cut off mid-sentence and plastered a smile on her face. I hoped I was the only one who could tell how fake it was.

Arnold stood in the doorway, surprise and delight etched into his features as my mom said, "Arnold, so good to see you again."

An awkward pause. I elbowed her gently, urging her to continue.

"I saw you returning to the motel earlier and was surprised to see you had stuck around," she said. "I'd assumed you'd left at the same time all the others did."

"I would have, except the police have new information that has led to them detaining all pilots and their crews. Shouldn't take more than a day or two to get this cleared up, then I'll be on my way to the Grand Canyon." He paused. "You could come with me, you know."

Arnold said it like this wasn't the first time he'd asked my mother to run away and join him on his national parks tour. My mom's jawline tightened, and I wondered if this invitation was the reason she hadn't wanted Arnold to know he was staying in the same motel as her. I felt guilty that I'd made her come over with me and promised myself I'd do something to make it up to her.

"Oh, Al, you know I can't abandon my daughter and her kids. I've told you, she's a single mom and can use all the help she can get. She's used to being a working mom—not always knowing where her kids are or what they're up to. She needs me to help keep an eye on things."

Never mind. I took my promise back, now that she was insinuating that I wasn't a good mom. Just because I wasn't home the second my kids returned from school, freshly baked cookies in the oven and a smile to greet them, didn't mean that I was neglectful. Lilly and Flash were both good kids, and they knew I loved them. I always dropped everything the second they needed me. What else did she want?

"I understand stubborn children," Arnold said, throwing a glance behind him into his room. I assumed that meant his two sons were there.

One of them appeared in the doorway, and my breath caught. It was the one who had helped my mom into the basket the previous evening. I didn't know how Arnold had been able to produce a son that looked like that, but he had done well.

"Stubborn, huh?" Arnold's son said. "Keeping you safe is our job. You'd have killed yourself in that balloon years ago if it weren't for us."

Arnold waved a hand through the air, like that tiny fact didn't matter. "Laurie, you've met my oldest son, Jeremiah."

"And this is...?" Jeremiah said, nodding toward me.

Arnold looked like he was surprised by my presence, his gaze finally landing on me. "Oh, this is..."

Even though we'd met, he apparently couldn't remember my name, and he waited for me to fill in the blank.

"Maddie," I said, reaching forward and shaking Jeremiah's hand. It was firm, and calloused. Most likely from handling the ropes of his dad's balloon for however many years. It sent a thrill up my spine, and I quickly let go.

He smiled. "You get dragged along for the ride too?"

"Actually, I'm the one doing the driving," I said, liking how that admission made Jeremiah's eyebrows pop up. "I feel so bad about what happened to Charles Reed and am interested in his story. It seems like he was a fascinating person."

A bit of a white lie, bordering on an outright fabrication.

"Don't let the girl fool you," Arnold said with a laugh. "Apparently Maddie is an expert at tracking down murderers. Caught herself one just last year. She and her kids are trying to catch Charles's murderer so the festival can continue. Of course, there won't be much left of it, but still, a noble endeavor."

Jeremiah studied me for a moment. "Kids, huh? Married?"

"Divorced."

The man was more interested in my marital status than

the fact that I'd caught a murderer the previous year, and I wasn't sure what to make of that. But for some reason, it made my cheeks heat up.

"I'm sorry to say that we won't be much help in your investigation," Arnold said. "Unfortunately, we can't tell you much about Charles Reed." He looked truly sorry for it. "Didn't know him all that well."

"Oh, I'm sorry, I must have been mistaken," I said. "I heard he'd been traveling all over the world with his balloon for several years now, and I assumed you all must be a fairly tight-knit community."

Jeremiah was the one who spoke up this time. "Just because he managed to convince unsuspecting fools to fly him around didn't mean he was a part of the community. The man never lifted a finger to help his crew, sitting back and ordering people around. Even tried to steal me from my own dad's crew and gave us a hard time when I refused."

My mom shook her head, like the thought disgusted her. "The more I hear about that man, the worse my opinion of him. It was probably a relief when you heard he'd died."

Arnold shared an indecipherable look with Jeremiah. "I can't say we'll miss him, but no one deserves to die by falling from his own balloon." He turned back to us. "Charles had a different pilot at every event, no one willing to put up with him longer than that, so I doubt Charles even knew his pilot's name, let alone what kind of man he was. Something like this was bound to happen eventually."

My defenses immediately rose, and before I thought better of it, I said, "Andy is as decent a man as they come. He didn't do this."

Arnold was quiet for a moment, studying me, and I wished that for once I'd been able to keep my mouth shut. "You know the pilot they're holding at the police station?" he finally asked.

"Well, no, not exactly," I said. "His reputation precedes him."

Arnold nodded, like he'd thought as much. "Reputation doesn't mean anything. It doesn't tell the truth of what lies in the soul. All it means is that this Andy person was very good at telling people what they wanted to hear. Take Charles Reed, for example. He was always flaunting his money, telling people of the charities he'd contributed to over the years. Told people that he hired more crew members than necessary, as well as a pilot, because he believed in giving good, honest folks jobs—helping them provide for themselves. Always raised himself up as a philanthropist. But really, he was covering up for his own laziness and the life of luxury that he'd always enjoyed. And covering the fact that he always took and never gave. There were never any charities. Only food and wine and women. And balloons, of course. Always the balloons. He thought more highly of himself than anyone else ever did."

Arnold didn't know of Charles Reed's true upbringing,

it seemed. I wondered if anyone did. Other than the locals. Interesting that Charles, or Chuck as Valerie called him, had bothered to come back home at all, knowing they could expose him for who he truly was.

Or maybe that was the point. Maybe he'd liked people to see what he'd made of himself—had had something to prove.

And maybe that had been what had gotten him killed.

11

I sat out by the deserted pool, my legs hanging over the edge. Was it the ideal thinking location? Not in the slightest. But at least I was alone. The kids were in their room—had said they wanted some time to themselves. My mom was taking an afternoon nap.

And that left me here, not knowing why we were still at the festival, and wondering how angry Ruby and Parker would be with me if instead of proving Andy's innocence, I actually helped prove his guilt.

My phone rang, and I picked it up.

"Twenty-four hours. That's all it took for you to leave, witness a murder, then promise Ruby you'd free her friend from jail. And I don't hear a word from you this entire time."

Trish. I hadn't even thought of catching her up to speed —I was a terrible friend. "I am so sorry. For everything. For my mom ordering you to stay home and take care of things. For my lack of communication. Phone reception is terrible here and—"

She cut me off. "No need to apologize. Just let me know what's going on. Are you seriously involved with another murder investigation? If Sheriff Potts finds out—"

"She knows."

A pause.

"Sorry?"

"Sheriff Potts is here and running the investigation. Apparently, she used to be with the state police, and the local authorities are less than equipped to handle the situation. She stepped in to help out. Not sure how happy the police chief is about that."

Trish chuckled on the other end of the line. "Bet she didn't love seeing you there."

I wasn't sure. At first, with my kids walking all over the crime scene, no, I didn't think she had. But she'd warmed up to me a bit more since being put in charge. Even seemed like she wanted my help. "She actually called me, asked me to check out a witness—wanted to see if I could get anything she'd missed."

"Awww, looks like you have a new best friend." Trish said it like I'd acquired a puppy who wouldn't stop following me. "I suppose that means I'll need to reschedule your appointments for the next couple of days, but I have to have you back here Wednesday at the latest.

The rest of the week is booked solid. Think you can solve the murder before then?"

I blew out a breath. Whether I could or not didn't matter. This wasn't my investigation, and the kids and I needed to get back. "I'll be back either way. I really shouldn't even be staying, but the kids are begging, of course. They have the idea that if we solve it fast enough, they'll still be able to see the hot air balloons. I doubt that's even a possibility at this point, but my mom has met a gentleman she seems to like, so she wants to stick around a bit too. At least she did. It was weird this morning. She found out he was staying in the same motel as us, and she freaked out, like she was only interested in him if they didn't get too personally involved."

"Your mom met a guy?" Trish laughed. "That has to be some man if he can keep up with your mom."

No kidding.

My phone beeped, letting me know I had a low battery. I glanced toward the motel and saw Jeremiah out on the balcony, watching me. "Hey, Trish, my phone is about to die. But I'll check in with you tomorrow."

"You'll bounce ideas off me, won't you? About who you think did it? Because with just me and Ava here, I'm going stir crazy. Ruby said it was a balloon guy who died. Fell right out of his basket. Any clues so far?"

I threw another glance toward Jeremiah. He was still watching me. Didn't even glance away when I looked right at him.

"Everyone knows Charles Reed, the victim, but everyone has a different version of the type of guy he was. There is a common thread, though. No matter which version they knew, they all hated him."

Arnold didn't know anything useful. He thought he'd seen through Charles Reed's lies, but he'd only been fed a different version of them.

Valerie certainly acted like she knew the real Charles Reed, or Chuck as she called him. And her version certainly rang of truth. So did the bitterness. I could absolutely see her capable of killing Charles.

But how could anyone other than Andy have killed him?

I hated to admit it, but he seemed the most likely to have done it.

The girlfriend, Casey McKinnon, knew more than she was telling. The events hadn't happened like she'd told the police and me. She'd lied, but why? What was she covering up? I supposed it was possible that she'd done it, with Andy's help, and they were covering for each other. But why would Andy stay silent on Casey's involvement, taking the fall for the murder?

Jeremiah had descended the stairs and was walking toward me. My heart rate picked up, and I tried to keep my voice even as I said, "Trish, it doesn't look good for Ruby's friend, but I'm going to do my best. Make sure she knows I'm trying, huh?"

"Of course. Call me if you learn anything new, okay?"

"Will do."

I hung up just as Jeremiah reached me, his hands shoved in his pockets, wearing an easy smile.

"Nice day for a swim," he said, nodding toward the empty pool.

I returned his smile. "Don't need water to sunbathe."

"And you apparently don't need a swimming suit, either."

I glanced down, noting my pants and long-sleeved top. "Apparently not."

Jeremiah laughed and raised a questioning eyebrow, eyeing the spot next to me. When I didn't immediately offer an invitation, he asked, "Mind if I join you?"

I wasn't sure why this man wanted to—he was too handsome for his own good, and he knew I had kids. I'd avoided dating since the divorce, assuming that men would run in the opposite direction when they found out I was a package deal, and with teenagers no less. But he seemed sincerely interested in spending time with me, so I nodded. "Be my guest."

I scooted over, as if to make room for him, which was ridiculous, because there wasn't another person around as far as I could see.

"That's quite some mother you have," Jeremiah said after he'd gotten situated next to me. He pulled one leg up into his chest, leaving the other to hang next to mine. As it swung, it occasionally bumped my leg and sent a thrill through me. I desperately attempted to not act like fifteen-year-old me, but it wasn't working. Just his presence made my breathing shallow.

"Yes," I said, trying to keep my words steady. "She's a force of nature. I'm impressed that your dad hasn't run away yet." She'd certainly had that effect on me. As soon as I'd been able, I'd run as quickly as I could. And it wasn't until I'd returned to Amor that I'd truly felt bad about that. Guilty, even. If there was any way I could help her be happy, I would. She deserved it after a lifetime of loneliness, and maybe that happiness had come in the form of Arnold, the hot air balloon pilot.

"It would take a lot more than your mother to scare him off. Truth be told, she seems like the type of woman who could keep up with him. But..." Jeremiah's gaze found the bottom of the pool.

"What?" Was he about to tell me that my mom wasn't good enough for his dad? The nerve. I'd already started planning how I was going to tell this Jeremiah guy what I thought of him coming down here to insult my family when he glanced back at me, and I saw something I hadn't expected.

Vulnerability.

"It's only been two years since my mom died," he said. "And I don't know if my brother and I are ready for Dad to move on. I mean, we're both adults and we understand how this works. My dad isn't getting any younger, and we can't always be around. But still—I've never been able to imagine him with anyone else. And our family—we look out for each other."

Oh. My anger immediately deflated, and I felt bad for jumping to conclusions—I should have known better, considering how often I was warning others against it in my counseling sessions.

"I never knew my dad," I said. "I've never imagined my mom being interested in someone, but only because she's always been alone."

Jeremiah chuckled and raked his fingers through his hair. "What a weird situation this is."

"That it is."

Jeremiah hesitated, then turned to me. "Especially because, if it weren't for them taking a liking to each other, I would be asking you if you'd go out to dinner with me."

My breath hitched, and I attempted to appear natural, like his words hadn't had any effect on me. "Is that right?"

"Sure. There's a steakhouse up the road a bit, a weird place with a huge dancing cow that lights up at night, but the food is good. It's up by the police station, actually. From what I hear, you're familiar with the area. Ran into my dad there this morning, didn't you?"

The reminder of why we were still here at this motel doused whatever attraction I might be feeling toward Jeremiah—and I wasn't admitting that I was feeling anything toward him. Not more than I would toward a general acquaintance or a friend. Someone like—

"There you are."

I turned quickly at the sound of the familiar voice. The man I'd just been thinking of.

Benji.

"Hey." I hoped the heat in my cheeks wasn't apparent. Nothing had happened between Jeremiah and me, and even if it had, it wasn't like there would be anything wrong with it. Benji and I were just friends. Best friends. Had been since we were kids.

So then why did I feel guilty right now?

"I tried calling," he said, his gaze panning between Jeremiah and me, as if he were trying to figure out if he had interrupted something.

I pulled my phone from my pocket. "That's weird because I was just talking to Trish and I didn't see any missed calls." The last of the battery had been used up, and the phone was dead. I held it up, as if to prove that his missed calls weren't my fault, and definitely not related to the man sitting next to me. "Sorry, forgot to charge it earlier."

Benji nodded, his gaze on Jeremiah, as if sizing him up. "I was just swinging by to see if you and the kids have plans for dinner. There's a great steak place up the road, and I thought you might want to join me."

I forced my gaze to remain on Benji and ignore Jeremiah's gaze that I felt boring into me. Ignore that I'd just been invited to the same steakhouse by two different men within the past five minutes.

But Jeremiah hadn't really invited me, merely said that

he would have. And he hadn't invited my kids like Benji had.

"That sounds great," I told Benji, getting to my feet. I brushed dirt off my pants. "I figured you would have headed back to Amor by now."

"Thought about it, but it didn't feel right leaving you, especially when you've managed to get yourself involved in another murder investigation. Someone has to protect you from yourself." He gave me a teasing smile, and I laughed.

"You know me so well."

Jeremiah got to his feet, reminding us of his presence. His expression made me uneasy as he studied me for a minute.

"You're Arnold's son, aren't you?" Benji said, taking a step back. Like he was trying to be pleasant but also keep distance between them. "I remember seeing you last night at the Balloon Glow. You helped Maddie's mom into the basket."

Jeremiah eyed Benji warily and grunted.

"From the stories your dad tells, you guys have been all over the world in all sorts of crazy situations with that balloon of yours," Benji said, his tone still light but his expression guarded. "You hot air balloon guys really watch out for each other. Keep each other safe. I like that."

"You sound like a detective who is trying to sound like he's not investigating," Jeremiah finally said. He threw a glance my way. "Both of you do. Like my dad said, we don't know anything."

He stalked off, not bothering to wait for us to respond.

Benji and I stood in silence for a moment, not quite knowing what to say. But then I burst into laughter.

"Do you think he's going to tell everyone that we're here investigating the murder?" I asked.

"If he does, that will make your job a lot harder. No one likes talking to someone they know is snooping." Benji was watching me with a slight smile, but it was also questioning. Like he was wondering if something had happened between Jeremiah and me.

It didn't really matter whether we'd had a moment or not. Because right now, I was with my best friend in the world, and he had promised me steak.

12

"Flash will never forgive us. You know that, right?" I took note of the dancing cow I'd been promised, prancing proudly with its udders on full display on top of the restaurant. It looked more like a weird exotic dance club than a steak restaurant.

Benji laughed. "He will if we get a few boxes to go. You did try to invite him and Lilly, and they turned you down. That's not your fault."

That wasn't exactly true. I'd knocked. And Lilly had answered, but when I'd opened my mouth to invite them out to dinner, I'd realized I'd need to invite my mom too. And frankly, I needed this time. Time that was my own. Because ever since quitting my university position and moving down to Amor, it seemed everyone owned my time except me. Everyone wanted a piece of it.

"I may have told them that you and I were going sight-seeing, but that I'd take care of dinner when I got back." An outright lie. Unless driving to see an exotic cow counted as sightseeing. It was certainly a sight, but maybe not one worth seeing. I'd been promised that the steak would be better than the decor.

Benji threw a glance my way, a questioning eyebrow raised. "Any reason you didn't want them to come along?"

"I don't know—I guess I just needed an hour where I could hear my own thoughts rather than someone talking over them." I slipped my hand through Benji's arm as we walked toward the front doors, and I gave it a reassuring squeeze. Except, those biceps were rock hard, and squeezing them was nearly impossible.

Wow.

It took a second for me to find my train of thought.

"If I would have invited them to dinner, the kids would have jumped into the back seat, and you would have ended up back there with them because my mom would need the front seat. And then she would have caught a glimpse of Arnold as we left and told him he should come along, or she'd have taken it one step further and knocked on his door and demanded he and both his sons follow us, because the more the merrier—I couldn't handle that right now. I don't even know what I'm still doing here, rather than in Amor where I belong. I guess I just needed...quiet."

Benji gave a thoughtful nod, but he seemed almost disappointed by my response. What had he expected, that I loved being a single mom? That I loved having to be everything to everyone, every moment of the day? I felt guilty thinking otherwise, but the truth was that I was exhausted. And the hand I'd been dealt in life was beginning to wear on me.

I loved my family. And I wanted to be my best for them.

That was why I hadn't told them where I was going.

So that I could continue to be what they needed.

But I didn't tell Benji all of this. I didn't need to weigh him down with all my feelings of inadequacy. Instead, I tilted my head and said, "What? You think I should have dragged the gang here with us?"

"No," Benji said quickly. We entered the restaurant, keeping him from saying more, and I was relieved to see that it looked, and smelled, like your typical steak restaurant. After we were seated and handed menus, Benji's gaze settled on me. "It's just, for a moment, I'd wondered if you'd not told your family where you were going because..." He looked uncomfortable, like he was trying to find a way to express what he wanted to say and was coming up short.

"What?" I pressed, though unsure if I should.

Benji squirmed in his seat. "It's just that you and I haven't spent much time alone together. You know, since you've been back. And... I don't know."

"Oh." I was unsure what else to say to that. Not sure

what he meant by the comment. We did stuff together all the time. Or we used to. I supposed there hadn't been as much of that since my return to Amor, considering that I now had two kids. A business. A mom with too much time on her hands.

"I don't see why that would be something I'd have to keep from them," I said, genuinely confused. "You're my best friend, and they know it. You're the most natural person for me to be here with."

The look of disappointment hadn't left and only seemed to settle in deeper. "Yes, we have always been best friends. I suppose that's enough for you, but a part of me thought—hoped..." Benji blew out a breath of frustration, and he shook his head. "It was stupid to think it would ever be more than that, especially after all these years. Everything we've gone through."

I stared, stunned. Benji had admitted earlier in the year that back when we'd been in high school, he'd been in love with me. But twenty years had passed since then. And it wasn't until that moment that I realized I had no idea what he'd done with those two decades, except become a handyman. No idea what he'd been through. What had led him here. And I'd never thought to ask.

I also felt anger, though. Frustration. That he would put me in this kind of situation. "Benji, I don't know what to say."

A woman walked up, and I gave her my drink order but

then realized it wasn't the waitress. It was Valerie, the receptionist from the motel.

"Oh, hi. Fancy meeting you here," I said, trying my best to smile, even though my insides felt like they were crumbling. How could Benji do that to me? He'd always been the one safe place I could go. No expectations. Just acceptance. And now he was changing the rules.

Valerie didn't return my smile. "I'm sorry, I don't mean to interrupt," she said. "But I just wondered if the rumors are true. Are you here investigating Chuck's murder? Is that why you didn't run home at the same time everyone else did?" Her gaze jumped to Benji and then back to me.

He seemed deep in thought, like he was having trouble focusing on the conversation.

"No, not in any formal capacity," I said, curious why Valerie seemed so nervous at the prospect. "I'm a psychologist and was hired to help a patient who had come to the festival. She asked me to stay until the investigation was resolved." As soon as I said it, I regretted sharing so much information with a stranger. I'd felt the need to justify my presence, and my rambling mouth had gotten the better of me. But it wasn't Valerie's business why I was here, and I should have just told her I'd stayed for personal reasons.

Of course, she would have just taken that as an admission that yes, I was here to investigate the murder.

"A psychologist. Interesting." Valerie turned to leave, not seeming convinced that I was who I'd said I was, then turned back. "You should probably know that there are some powerful people who really don't want this murder to turn any messier than it has. They advise you to walk away, if you know what's good for you."

Benji sat up straighter, the conversation now having his full attention. "Excuse me, but did you just threaten us?"

Valerie gave a vigorous shake of her head. "Not me. I don't really care one way or the other. But that can't be said of other interested parties. I've been advised that I said too much when we chatted yesterday in the office, and I don't want to see anyone else hurt. Like I said, go back home if you know what's good for you."

And then Valerie disappeared through the back of the restaurant.

I was no longer concerned whether Benji saw himself as my best friend or the potential for more. Because no matter what he was, or who'd he become, I needed him.

I needed Benji.

He must have seen the fear that had clenched my stomach, and he slid out of his side of the booth and onto mine. Placing an arm around my shoulders, he pulled me in.

"I'm sure it was nothing. Just a scare tactic."

I leaned my head on his shoulder and pulled in shallow breaths. I could feel Benji's heartbeat. It was racing. Maybe even faster than my own. As much as he wanted to help reassure me of my and my family's safety, he'd only succeeded in reassuring me of one thing.

That I needed to solve this murder. And fast.

I straightened, armed with new resolve. Beni's arm fell from my shoulders, and he watched me with curiosity and concern.

When my gaze met his, I said, "We need to find out what happened in that basket."

I REMEMBERED Jeremiah telling me that the restaurant was close to the police station, so it only took a couple of minutes to drive over. I knew it was getting late, but someone had to be there. It wasn't like police work was a nine-to-five kind of job.

"You're sure about this?" Benji asked, his gaze darting around, like he thought someone could be watching.

Who knew, maybe someone was.

The thought sent chills through me, and I wrapped my arms around my stomach to keep warm.

"No," I said. "But I'm not going to stand by while an innocent man sits behinds bars and my family is threatened. What kind of person would I be if I ran back home, too scared to stand up for what is right?"

"You don't know that Andy is innocent," Benji said, which surprised me, considering he had seemed convinced of this fact not too long ago. Maybe he was scared too and saying what he felt he must to get me to leave.

"If he were guilty, there wouldn't be some powerful

person using Valerie as a mask, warning us to stay away. If the police had their person, there would be no reason."

Benji didn't seem to have a rebuttal for that, knowing it was a fair point, and instead followed me inside the station.

An officer sat behind the desk just inside the front doors, and I approached him, hoping I appeared more confident than I felt.

"I'd like to speak to your guest, Andy," I told him. Was guest the right term? Prisoner sounded so harsh.

The officer watched me from behind bushy eyebrows. "Does this *guest* have a last name?" He seemed slightly amused.

"I'm sure he does, but it escapes me at the moment."

Had I ever known Andy's last name? Yes, I had written it down. But I couldn't remember for the life of me what it was.

The officer watched me for another second, seeming intrigued, then said, "Sorry, no visitors."

I balked. "If you're going to have him behind bars, the least you can do is give him a little social interaction. I'm not asking you to release him." I'd already tried that, and it hadn't worked. "I'm a friend of his, and I just want to make sure he's doing all right."

"Yeah, we're friends of his," Flash piped up from behind me. I closed my eyes, counting to ten, attempting calm breaths. When I opened them, my mother and Lilly had joined him.

What were they doing here? One glance at Benji told me that he was as confused as I was. This had turned into a whole family affair, and Valerie's warnings played on repeat in my mind. The fear returned.

Not only was this going to look really bad if someone was indeed watching, but it was going to make getting in to talk to Andy more difficult. And I really needed to talk to him.

"All of you want to see our murderer?" the officer asked, incredulous.

"You have no proof he did it," my mom said, walking up with an angry stride. "It's a wrong place, wrong time kind of situation, and you know it. You just don't have anyone else, so you're laying blame wherever you can."

"Excuse me? Are you telling me that we are not only incompetent at our jobs, but that we are dishonest, as well?" The officer got to his feet, his eyes angry.

At this rate, we were either going to end up in the crosshairs of the real murderers or as Andy's cellmates.

"We would never presume to think such a thing," I said quickly, shooting my mom an annoyed glance. "They can all stay out here. I'd just like to talk to Andy—check on him. Please."

The officer seemed to soften for a slight moment, but then hardened back up. "No."

He then sat back down at his desk and started typing on his computer, an obvious signal that he was finished speaking with us.

"Thanks a lot," I murmured to my mom as I turned away.

"What? It's not my fault they run an inhuman racket here, not even allowing visitors," she said, loudly enough that I was sure the officer had heard.

There was no way we were getting in now.

"How did you even know that Benji and I were here?"

Lilly snorted. "Please. Sightseeing? You were obviously going out to investigate without us. It wasn't difficult to figure out where you'd go."

Guilt settled in my stomach because investigating had been the furthest thing from my mind. Steak and Benji had been all that had occupied it. Being alone. Without family. Without complications.

Of course, then there had been nothing but complications.

My thoughts were interrupted when Sheriff Potts strode in from the back with an exasperated look on her face. Her presence was either going to be very good or very bad for us. It was difficult to tell which. "Do you always insult people when you need something from them?" she asked.

My mom placed a hand on her hip. "Only when they are being arrogant and power hungry." Once again, her words were loud enough for the entire station to hear.

I groaned. "Mom, will you stop? You're going to get yourself arrested."

"For what? There's such thing as freedom of speech," she

said, folding her arms across her chest and throwing a glare in the officer's direction. His gaze met hers, and he didn't look away, his lips in a tight line. "You should be doing everything you can to find out the truth about this murder," she continued. "Not just trying to get the paperwork done so you can attempt to salvage this year's festival. Which isn't happening, by the way, because you might have the pilots and their crews hanging around, but you don't have a single attendee left."

Sheriff Potts looked to me for help. Maybe she had a muzzle in the back we could use.

"You may have forgotten that I don't live here," the sheriff said, turning back to my mom. "I couldn't care less about the festival. I have experience with murder investigations, which is the only reason I'm still here. Otherwise, I'd already be back in Amor. I can't believe I'm going to say this, but your little hometown is a vacation compared to this place. Trust me, the truth is all I care about."

This was my chance.

"So, you'll take me back to talk to Andy, then?"

The sheriff eyed me warily. "You know something, don't you?"

I raised a shoulder, like maybe I did, maybe I didn't. "I haven't been able to get his side of the story, which is kind of an important one. Especially since Casey is lying about what happened in the balloon basket that night."

Sheriff Potts hesitated, but then nodded. "All right. But I can't take your mom. Or the kids. Just you and Benji."

"I completely agree."

That resulted in a lot of protests, but my family was an unpredictable lot, and if they tagged along, the only thing I was going to gain was being thrown out and banned from the police station. And that was saying something, considering most people wanted out.

The police station was smaller than I'd realized, and all it took was walking through one unlocked door to where a single cell sat. A man lay on a cot, and it looked like he was sleeping. He was large enough that he took up the entire space, one leg hanging off.

"Andrew, you have visitors."

Andy stirred, as if he'd been wakened, but it seemed fake—like he'd been awake the whole time. Listening. I was certain he'd heard every word my mom had shouted in the lobby.

As he got to his feet, I tried to smother my surprise. Andy was not what I had expected. He was tall. Bald. Huge arms. If it weren't for his eyes, I'd probably have thought him capable of murder. It wouldn't have been difficult for him to toss Charles Reed overboard. Could probably have done it one-handed.

But those eyes. They were troubled. And kind. Even though the rest of his expression was pulled into a serious frown, his eyes smiled.

"Benji, it's been a while," Andy said. "It's always good of you to come out and see us."

"Wasn't about to miss this one. Parker said it was going to be something special."

Andy gave a slow nod. "He had high hopes for the race this year. Said he had a lucky charm."

"Ruby?" I guessed.

Andy's gaze found me. It was calculating, and it made me want to step behind Benji so he couldn't find whatever he was looking for. "I was shocked when I saw he'd invited a woman along for the festival," he finally said. "Never done that before, but after seeing her jump into action when Parker's balloon went down, I could see why he liked her."

Benji stepped forward and grabbed one of the bars. "What happened at the Balloon Glow, Andy? Why were you even still here, let alone piloting for another guy?"

Sheriff Potts cleared her throat, and Benji took a step back.

Andy threw a glance her way. "Mind stepping out for a moment, ma'am? It's hard to talk when I know you're making a mental note of everything I say. Regardless of how relevant, or not, it is to your case against me."

The sheriff hesitated, but then made eye contact with me. I knew what it meant. She expected a full report when we were done.

I gave a little nod, and she left.

Once the door had clicked shut, my full attention returned to Andy. He was watching me carefully, like he'd seen the acknowledgement that had occurred between the sheriff and me.

He must have determined that I could still be trusted, though, because he said, "I never should have agreed to be that man's pilot. And I'm going to regret it every day for the rest of my life. Even if I manage to get out of this jail cell. But I better start at the beginning."

13

Andy rubbed a hand over his smooth head, like just thinking about what he had to tell us was stressing him out. "Charles Reed was not a good man, I'm going to just put that out there. Horrible guy. I'd known him years ago when he was a crew member for some pretty prominent ballooners. He spent more time schmoozing than doing his actual job. Don't get me wrong, the guy knew his way around a balloon. Knew how to fly one too. He would have been a fantastic pilot if he'd put his mind to it. Instead, all he cared about was making connections. Either the pilots didn't have enough brains to notice, or more likely, they didn't care. They were rich. They liked the attention. I think Charles was more of a pet to them. Either way, they must have noticed how smart the guy was because they brought him in on some business deals, and next thing you know, the guy has a ridiculous amount of money."

"How long ago was that?" I asked.

Andy looked up at the ceiling, like he had to think about it. "Maybe about five years ago. Anyway, none of us had liked him much when he was crew, and we liked him a lot less once he had his own balloon. The guy was smart and talented, well spoken—and yet he wouldn't lift a finger when it came to flying in the festivals. Never competed in any of the competitions—just smiled and waved, like his presence was a gift. The act worked on the lady folks, unfortunately. One of the many reasons none of us ever brought women to the festivals. Those who did regretted it." Andy's expression darkened. It only lasted a moment, then it cleared, and he glanced at me. "Until this year, that is. Rafael and I were both shocked that Parker had brought Ruby."

Benji leaned against the wall. "I remember you and Rafael complaining about Charles a couple of years back. I hadn't made the connection that it was the same guy. You mean to tell me that this was the man who—"

"Yeah." Andy's tone was sharp, as if letting Benji know that this was not a topic that was up for discussion. I would definitely be asking Benji more about that later.

"What on earth were you doing piloting for him?" Benji sounded incredulous, like whatever Charles Reed had done to Andy, it had been bad.

Andy released a long breath, then slumped onto the cot, burying his head in his hands.

"I needed the money," he finally said. "And Charles knew it. I work for a startup company that looked like it had a lot of promise, but it isn't doing so well. Doing these festivals has been keeping me afloat while I figure out my next move. It doesn't help that I enjoy the casinos."

"You have a gambling problem," Benji bluntly said in translation.

Andy raised a shoulder. "Like I said, I enjoy it. Anyway, when Parker and Rafael took off, I no longer had a balloon to be a crewmate for. Parker's balloon is damaged and will take a while to repair. When Charles approached me, he must have been able to tell how desperate I was. And he was offering me a lot more money as pilot than I've been making as Parker's crewmate. More than he should have, to be honest. But as much as I hated the guy, who was I to turn down an opportunity like that?"

"He hired you the day of the Balloon Glow?" I asked, remembering that Parker and Ruby had left just that afternoon. "Isn't that a bit short-sighted on his part, not already having a pilot lined up?"

Andy grimaced. "He had one, but his pilot didn't last the full first day."

"And you still took the job?" Benji asked, shaking his head.

"You don't get to come in here and judge my choices," Andy said, anger accenting his words. "I told you I regret it.

If Parker hadn't been stupid and taken his balloon up midday because he needed alone time," he did air quotes around *alone time*, "then he wouldn't have crashed, and I'd be chasing his balloon in the truck with Rafael rather than sitting here in a jail cell for something I didn't do."

I softened my tone, hoping to placate Andy. He'd stood from the cot and was now pacing the cell like a caged tiger. I didn't want to agitate him any more than he already was.

"What happened up there?" I asked. "We know you didn't kill Charles, but you have to admit that you're in a terrible position to prove it. You're the only one strong enough to lift him."

Benji gave me a warning look as Andy's gaze snapped to me.

"So, you think I did it? Think I chose to go up in that balloon, just so I could kill the guy?" Andy leaned against the wall. "Trust me, I wanted to. Everyone did. Do you know how he treated his employees? Brought all that food and drink in the balloon, and I was warned not to go near it. Wasn't allowed to bring my own stuff and wasn't allowed to touch his. The food and wine was for Charles Reed and his girlfriend. Not that she ate any. Apparently, she's on a strict diet, and pretty much everything Charles had was off limits, including his wine. From the looks of it, he didn't mind one bit. Not the way he was guzzling from the bottles all evening. My only job was to have my focus one hundred percent on the task at hand."

"Okay," I said, trying to piece together what had

happened that night. "So, Charles Reed is drunk, smiling and waving at everyone, passing out his trading cards. You're keeping the balloon at the right height, and his girl-friend, Casey, is what, just enjoying the evening?"

Andy gave a small nod. "Pretty much."

"And then what happened?"

Andy's gaze dropped, and he became squeamish. The man couldn't stay still, folding his arms, unfolding them, then folding them again.

"Andy?" Benji said, his voice quiet. "We can't help you if you don't tell us everything."

Andy gave a small nod. "Charles Reed didn't die from falling from the basket. He was already dead."

14

I couldn't have heard right. Because if I had, I'd swear that Andy had just said that Charles Reed had been dead before he'd ever fallen from the basket, let alone when he'd hit the ground.

Benji looked just as shocked as I felt. "I'm sorry?"

Andy looked miserable at the thought of having to tell us what had happened that night. "Charles told me he wasn't feeling so well and thought he might call it a night. His hand was on his chest, and he seemed to be having trouble breathing. Casey wasn't even paying attention, leaning over the basket and waving at someone she knew. She was being all sappy and telling them what a beautiful night it was and kept going on about the stars and how there were so many that it seemed they could just swallow us whole."

"How much wine had Charles drunk at that point?" I asked.

"Nearly two bottles. He'd brought five." Andy pushed off from the wall and sat back down on the cot. It creaked under his large frame. "Charles really wasn't looking good, and I was about to tell the crew that we were quitting for the night. Even had my phone out to call the paramedics. That was when I realized I'd somehow picked up Rafael's phone instead of mine. Before I could figure out how to use the emergency setting on his phone, the balloon started lifting. I dropped the phone and opened the flap to help bring the balloon down, but when Charles collapsed on the bottom of the basket, I abandoned my efforts and instead gave him CPR."

That explained why no one had been able to get ahold of Rafael. Wherever he was, his phone was here in evidence.

"What was Casey doing this whole time?" I asked.

Andy snorted. "Freaking out. I told her to call 911, but she was beside herself—inconsolable. Women like that are only good for one thing, if you know what I mean."

I started, not believing Andy had just said that. It must have shown in my expression because Andy's lips parted, like he had surprised himself.

"I'm sorry—I didn't mean that. I mean I did, but I have the utmost respect for women. Really. It's just, I needed help. And all she could do was curl up in a ball, hands over her ears, crying. I mean, honestly, do you know what it's like flying into the night, a man dying, and someone is shrieking in your ear?"

"Sounds stressful," Benji said, seemingly trying to bring things back on track.

I pulled in a long breath. Just because my opinion of Andy had dropped a point or two didn't mean that I needed to let his opinion of women affect how I looked at the facts of that night. We needed all the information we could get before the sheriff returned to kick us out.

Speaking of which, it had been a while since she'd left.

My gaze found a camera mounted in the corner of the room. And if I had to guess, there was probably a microphone somewhere as well.

That was why she was allowing us to stay with Andy, alone. Because she'd been listening in this whole time.

It was just as well, I supposed. And now that we had gotten this far, I wanted to finish it.

"You have no idea," Andy mumbled with a shake of his head. "I don't understand how he went from drinking wine to lying dead in the basket."

"But why didn't you tell the police this?" I asked, not understanding why he'd let them assume Charles Reed had died from falling from the basket rather than from a sudden illness.

"Casey. She stopped crying long enough to tell me that we'd be blamed—that they would think it was us. But that if Charles fell from the basket, they'd assume that was how he'd died. It wasn't murder because he was already dead."

Benji stepped toward the jail cell. "And you went along with it?"

"Of course not," Andy said, looking offended that Benji would dare think so low of him. "I know she's small and overly emotional, but that woman is tough. Turns out Casey competes in weightlifting—and wins. Not only that, but she's really connected—dad's a congressman or something—and she was terrified of how her involvement would reflect on him and how it could ruin his career. There was a lot of motivation for her to get Charles's body to disappear. And she did. Single-handed. I couldn't believe it. No one else did, either. Which is why I'm in here, and she's out there."

His story did seem a bit far-fetched. But as I studied him, it seemed he was telling the truth.

"That must have made you angry," I said, taking on my therapist tone.

"Of course it did. But what am I going to do about it? I'm a nameless guy from the Midwest—no connections and no money. Just a guy trying to make a few bucks here and there. No one is coming to rescue me. No band of fancy lawyers."

Maybe this was why Ruby had asked me to help Andy out. Maybe she and Parker had known he didn't stand a chance without someone on his side.

And apparently that person was me.

"Maybe not, but you do have friends. And we're going to prove that you didn't murder Charles Reed. No one did.

He was dead upon arrival. A freak illness that no one could have predicted. And we're going to prove it."

BENJI and I had never managed to order drinks, let alone our steak, before rushing out to the police station.

"I feel like I owe you an apology," I told him as we left the holding area. "I dragged you into this mess, and here it is, eight-thirty, and you haven't eaten dinner yet."

"I don't mind," Benji said, giving me a smile that said I should know better than to think his involvement was an imposition. "Andy is my friend, and I want to help him too."

My thoughts went to the little time we'd had at the restaurant. "And I need to apologize for making things awkward at the restaurant." I paused. "It's not like I haven't thought of what might happen if we were more than friends. But we're different people than we were twenty years ago. I have no idea what you've done with yourself over the past couple of decades, and I barely recognize myself. I'm not the same carefree girl I was, and no one deserves to have to deal with the amount of baggage I'm carrying."

Benji held up a hand to stop me, knowing I was in full ramble mode. Because, no matter how much we'd both changed, he still knew me. And that thought was comforting.

"You don't need to apologize. I was feeling insecure,

and it was me who sprang things on you. It's me who is sorry. I never meant to make you uncomfortable. Can we rewind and pretend our attempt at dinner tonight never happened?"

That thought didn't feel any better.

Before I could explore why, though, my mom intercepted us in the lobby. "Well, what happened?"

I threw an uneasy glance around the police station. "We'll talk more when we get back to the motel. Suffice to say, there's more to this situation than meets the eye."

Because if what Andy was saying was true—if Charles Reed had died from natural causes—then why were Benji and I being threatened to stop investigating further?

I WAS STARVING, and Benji wouldn't admit it, but I knew he must be too. Flash had no problem announcing that he was dying from hunger and would most likely waste away before we'd made it back to the motel.

It only seemed fair that Benji and I grab dinner for everyone from the restaurant and meet the family back at the motel, where we'd all eat steak while sitting on the floor, because there was only room for one at the small desk the motel provided.

Of course, we hadn't realized that the restaurant didn't do to-go orders and ended up having to pretend that two people really did want enough food for five people. As soon as we received it, we asked for it to be boxed up, which, it turned out, was a grave sin. They didn't want to be treated like a fast-food restaurant—their establishment was one of reputation. Which meant that, once we had our food, we were politely asked to not return.

I'd never been banned from a business of any kind before, and funnily enough, I found it exhilarating.

"Do you think our names are on some sort of permanent record?" I asked Benji, sincerely hoping they were. Maybe it was a midlife crisis, but I was suddenly feeling rebellious.

That was before we'd arrived back at the motel with all our food. Before we'd heard the latest news.

As soon as we arrived, bags in hand, Flash threw open the door, a wide grin taking up most of his face.

At first, I thought it was at the prospect of dinner, but then, breathless, Flash said, "Mr. Reed didn't die from the fall."

Benji and I exchanged nervous glances.

"We know that," I said. But how did Flash know that? I hadn't told them anything we'd discovered yet.

I stepped into the kids' room, and Benji followed. Lilly was sitting on one of the beds, cross-legged, looking through the pictures on her camera. Flash had some sort of document pulled up on his computer and ushered us over.

"What do you have there?" I stepped toward the computer but didn't walk all the way to the desk. It was better that I not know what website he was on and what information he was accessing.

"The internet is terrible in this place, and it keeps cutting out, or I would have been able to access these files sooner," Flash said, sliding into the chair and scrolling through the webpage he was on. "But they ran a toxicology report on Charles Reed, not sure why. Must have suspected something, though. Turns out they were right. There was strychnine in his system. Enough to kill him, for sure."

I had no idea what strychnine was or where someone would get something like that. But that was certainly not death by natural causes.

That was murder.

And it certainly didn't prove Andy's innocence.

"Strychnine," Benji said, rubbing an eyebrow. "That isn't stuff you want to mess around with. Mostly illegal now, except for its use as a pesticide. It's odorless, though, and you could add it to someone's drink or their food easily enough."

There had been plenty of that in the basket. And once again, Andy and Casey had had easy access.

"How long does it take for symptoms to set in?" I asked Benji.

He gave me an amused smirk. "I know enough to stay away from the stuff, but I never bothered to see what might happen if I tried to kill someone with it."

I laughed. "Sorry if I implied otherwise."

Flash's fingers were already flying over the keyboard.

"Wouldn't take more than thirty minutes, if it was a big enough dose. Maybe even less. Looks like it affects the respiratory system—makes it so he wouldn't be able to breathe."

What an awful way to go.

"But he would have had to have been given it before the balloon took flight."

Benji nodded. "Neither Casey nor Andy was affected, but we already know they didn't eat or drink Charles's food and wine. That must have been how it was administered. Andy said that Charles had already drunk two bottles on his own."

It was possible someone knew that Charles wouldn't allow Andy to partake of his personal food stash and also that Casey was on a diet. That would ensure the poison would only affect Charles.

Lilly glanced up from her camera. "You know, there's something unusual about the wine."

I walked over to the bed and looked over her shoulder at her camera. "What do you mean?"

Lilly pointed to a picnic basket that sat in one corner of the balloon basket. "All the food was in there. Flash ate some of it, so we know that hadn't been poisoned. It had to have been the wine. But there's no way Charles could have drunk five bottles of wine on his own, so why are there five empty bottles?"

My heart stalled. I had totally forgotten Flash's pockets stuffed with food from the crime scene. If the murderer had decided to poison the food instead of the wine...no, I couldn't let my mind go there. Flash was fine. He was okay. This time.

But I would be having a very serious conversation with him about where he acquired his midnight snacks from now on.

"I suppose one possibility is that Andy wasn't telling the truth about him and Casey not drinking Charles's wine," Benji said. "But they weren't poisoned." He joined me at Lilly's bed and scooted in close so he could see the picture. As he did, his cologne washed over me. Had he ever worn cologne before? I'd never noticed.

"There weren't any glasses that I saw, which means Charles was probably drinking straight from the bottle. I would never let other people drink straight from my bottle like that," Lilly said. "Flash is always trying to get me to share my soda. But all that backwash? Gross."

I agreed. The only one drinking my backwash was me.

"Maybe no one drank the remaining wine," I said. I had a theory. But I didn't know how to prove it. Couldn't go throwing out wild ideas to the sheriff—she hadn't appreciated that in the past. "What if the poison had been injected into all five bottles, and someone wanted to get rid of the evidence?"

"There would still be enough in the bottles to test it for poison, right?" Flash said. "I'm assuming it only takes a few drops. The killer should have thrown everything out, including the bottles."

That was a good point. "Maybe they were interrupted. Better yet, maybe they had no idea which bottle the poison was in. Let's say you're adding poison to a stash of wine, and you only got through two bottles before someone walks in. You act like you're packing up a picnic basket, and now you have no idea which bottles the poison is in. After Charles's death, they knew that one of the poisoned bottles was drunk from, but which one of the other bottles held the poison? They now needed to get rid of the rest of the wine. But with all the chaos and the police, maybe they only had the chance to dump the wine before the area was closed off."

A knock on the door.

Benji answered it, but I'd already known it would be my mom on the other side of the door.

She stood in the doorway, and with one glance around the room, she guessed exactly what we were up to.

"I'm gone for a ten-minute nap, and this is what happens?" she asked, bustling in. "If you're going to launch a full murder investigation, the least you could do is invite your mother. This is a family trip, after all." She settled herself onto Flash's bed. "What did I miss?"

15

I knew to expect Sheriff Potts at some point. With the cameras in the cell, what we'd said couldn't stay quiet forever. I'd half thought she'd stop us from leaving the police station the previous evening, but we'd left unhampered.

Of course, the sheriff must have known by now about the poison in Charles's system. Whoever had poisoned the wine must have not really cared if it took out both Charles and his girlfriend, as long as it got its target. Thank goodness Andy hadn't been allowed any of the wine. Not that you probably wanted a drunk pilot, even if you were just sitting on the ground.

The knock on the door came too early by my mom's standards, but at eight-thirty, I'd already been up for a couple of hours, my mind racing.

"Sheriff, what a pleasant surprise," I said, opening the

door and letting her in. "I'm assuming this is about our visit with Andy last night. Nice guy. Completely innocent, of course."

The sheriff gave me an amused smile. "So, you believe him."

"Why shouldn't I? It makes sense. Remember when I described Charles falling from the basket? He wasn't flailing or anything—just dropped."

Sheriff Potts made herself comfortable in the over-stuffed chair in the corner, like this was her room too. She certainly seemed a lot more relaxed around me lately. That was a good sign. Or it meant that she'd given up and no longer felt the need to be professional. I hoped it wasn't the latter.

"As much fun as this is, I'm going to need to have Maddie catch me up on the details later," my mom said, picking up her purse. Because despite her complaints about the early hour, she had a breakfast date. With Arnold. Said it was my fault for exposing where we were staying when we'd questioned him and his sons the day before, but she didn't exactly seem sad about it. In fact, my mom was practically glowing, and she hadn't stopped smiling since she'd woken that morning.

As soon as she'd left and the door closed, Sheriff Potts turned her attention to me.

"It does make sense," she said. "As far as the part about Charles Reed falling ill, we did find quite a bit of strychnine in his system. Could have been added to the wine by

Andy, you know. He had plenty of opportunity while they were the only ones in the basket. And five bottles? Seems like someone was intent on getting Charles drunk, and then some."

"Why would Andy do that? He has no motive."

Sheriff Potts cocked an eyebrow. "You mean other than the fact that Charles had an affair with Andy's sister, broke up her marriage, then dumped her a week after she left her husband? I'm assuming Andy blames himself, considering that he'd been the one to invite her out to the festival. This was three or four years ago, so he may not have been aware of Charles's reputation, poor guy."

I stared. This had been the big thing that Benji had never gotten around to telling me.

And now Andy had both motive *and* opportunity.

"It could have been added to the wine by anyone, and Andy was too visible," I said, ignoring the fact that things were looking worse for Andy than ever. "It was probably someone who was around when Charles was packing up the picnic basket."

"Charles would never pack his own basket. Casey?"

"Or a crew member. There were plenty of them—more than what Charles actually needed, according to our motel's desk clerk, Valerie. He liked to give jobs to people in the community. Of course, now I'm thinking it was a power play. But either way, there were a lot of people who had access to Charles's food."

Sheriff Potts leaned back in the chair and closed her

eyes, like she'd woken up tired. Or maybe never gone to bed. "I need to get out of here, Maddie. This town, I mean. I'm so tired of the same old scene. The officers here are just as anxious to send me on my way as I am. If we do solve this murder, there won't be accolades or a party. There will be relief that I'm finally out of their hair."

"It must be hard to be a woman in your profession."

She snorted. "That's putting it lightly. But it's also not the biggest challenge. I was with the state police before I came to your town. I'm sure you might have guessed that I didn't volunteer for the transfer. Amor had a problem. Their sheriff had retired, and no one had any interest in taking his place, nor does your town have the money for their own police department. Can't have a town with no law enforcement. And no one felt it was their responsibility to rectify the problem."

I wanted to ask Sheriff Potts what that had to do with her, but she seemed lost in thought, and I didn't want to interrupt. If I did, she may clam up and never speak of this again.

"It wasn't my fault," she said softly. "The guy wouldn't leave me alone. Everywhere I went, he seemed to show up. They said I'd been stalking him—that I had a vendetta. Because he'd been the one who sold my sister the drugs that killed her. Did I hate him? Yes. Did I want to catch him in the act so I could be the one to arrest him? Again, yes. But I hadn't been following him. It was the other way around. He kept putting himself in dangerous situations.

Wanted me to think he was up to something that he wasn't. You know what happened the day before he died?"

I stayed silent, sure it was a rhetorical question. I wondered how long Sheriff Potts had had all this building up—how long she'd wanted to talk to someone about all this. Whatever had happened, she'd needed help. Not a transfer.

"He yelled at me from across the street. Maybe not at me, exactly, but loud enough for me to hear. I knew it was for my benefit. Wanted everyone to know that he was stealing the car, just for the fun of it. Said he knew for a fact that it belonged to a drug dealer and that the guy had a stash hidden in the trunk. I don't know what he expected me to do—I'd given up on arresting him weeks before then. I'd fallen into his trap so many times, we were on a first-name basis. He liked getting me into trouble. Would claim he was just standing there and that I demanded a body search for no reason, and stuff like that. I ran the plates later, and it turned out that the car was his."

The sheriff fell silent.

"Do you think he felt guilty?" I finally asked. I didn't expect Sheriff Potts to answer, but she opened her eyes and gave me a small nod.

"Yeah. I didn't find out until later that he was my sister's boyfriend. He wasn't just a drug dealer, though he was certainly that as well. I never saw him carrying drugs after my sister overdosed—never saw another transaction. Just him following me around, begging for my attention. Telling my boss on me."

"He was trying to make you mad so you would what, lose your temper and shoot him?"

Sheriff Potts' gaze landed anywhere but on me. "The day he died, he finally confronted me. Apologized for lying to my boss about me and getting me in trouble. He asked why I hadn't killed him already. He said that I knew what he'd done to my sister. That I knew he didn't deserve to live. He wanted to know what was taking me so long."

She pulled in a shuddered breath.

"And that's when I saw him for the scared kid he was. The one that was so desperate and filled with such anguish that he was begging me to take his life."

If that was the day he'd died, then...

"I didn't even see him coming," the sheriff said. "I drove away and never realized what his plan was until he'd already flung himself in the way of the car. The kid didn't stand a chance."

I sat there, stunned. "There were cameras on your car, right? They knew it wasn't your fault."

She gave a slow nod. "My dash cam showed that he had thrown himself in front of the car. But a security camera from a nearby parking lot had also captured my conversation with the boy. It had no sound, so they saw what looked like an argument. What looked like the boy pleading with me. They thought I'd instructed him to do it

—to end his life that way. As punishment for what he did to my sister. That I had threatened him."

"But they couldn't prove it."

"No. They could have made up some excuse to fire me, but they didn't want to deal with the fallout of what that might mean. Didn't want the media to catch wind and have to answer questions they didn't want to address. So they gave me two options: I quit my job, or I run for sheriff."

Wow. We'd all speculated on what might have brought Sheriff Potts to town, but it hadn't been that.

"So you're just biding your time, keeping your nose clean, until your term is up so you can get a job somewhere else. Somewhere far away from New Mexico?"

"Something like that. It's nothing against your town, but I need a fresh start. I need a break. Thought it would be fun to get away this weekend, make some extra money while seeing the balloons. It would have been the closest thing to a vacation that I've had in years." The sheriff managed a wry smile. "Some vacation, huh? There must be someone in my old department who found out I was here and thought it would be funny to assign me to a murder, considering that's what they thought I'd done. Still making me pay my penance."

I didn't understand why people were always so intent on tearing others down rather than lifting them up. What was it about human nature that put us in constant survival mode—the belief that for us to win, someone else had to fail? And even when someone had failed, the need to kick them while they were down, just to make sure they would stay down.

That was not the type of world I wanted to live in. Years ago, when I'd been trying to decide on a major in college, I'd thought that as a psychologist I could make a difference one person at a time.

But there were moments when I wondered if it was all futile—that the world had gone crazy, and there was nothing I could do about it.

"Well, the joke will be on them," I said. "When you solve this murder, it will be another gold star on your record."

Sheriff Potts surprised me by releasing the loudest laugh I'd heard in a long time, not to mention from someone I'd never actually seen laugh.

"I'm sorry," she said, wiping a tear from laughing too hard. "I think the stress is getting to me. But I had the mental picture of all of us state officers with charts like you'd see in a kindergarten classroom, and the chief walking around handing out stars to his prize officers." Her smile dipped. "Of course, there will always be those whose charts are empty. Who desperately wish they'd be recognized for their hard work, even if it's not as obvious as the others."

Oh, man. The sheriff had some deep-seated issues, things that she'd probably been avoiding for years. And now it was all forcing itself to the surface, and I doubted it would slow anytime soon. The faucet had been turned on, the handle broken off, and it just needed to run its course.

I tried to glance at my phone discreetly, noting the time. I'd wanted to sneak out while my mom was at break-fast to talk with some of Charles's crew members, see if anyone had noticed anything of value the night of his murder. Apparently, Charles had put them all up in the same hotel as Casey, and I'd been worried about making it inside the hotel, relying on the fact that I wouldn't have the rest of my family with me, so maybe security wouldn't recognize me.

Listening to Sheriff Potts, though, it seemed that having law enforcement with me might be a better way to go.

"You're right, you don't get the credit you deserve," I told the sheriff.

"It's not credit I want," Sheriff Potts insisted. "It's respect. The chance to make a difference—not always feeling like I'm being held back."

"And you feel like being forced into the position of sheriff is keeping you from meeting your potential."

The sheriff hesitated. "You have a nice little town there. You do. But it isn't what I envisioned for myself."

I understood that, and Sheriff Potts certainly couldn't be faulted for it.

"Then we'd better catch this murderer so you can get your career back on track."

"We?"

I thought it humorous that she still thought she needed to put on a front—pretend that we weren't working this murder together, even as she was feeding me tips and asking what I'd found in return.

"I'm assuming you've been out to talk with Charles's crew."

Sheriff Potts nodded. "But that was when we'd assumed Charles had been pushed out of the balloon. I haven't been out to the hotel since then. From what I understand, they're living the high life on Charles's tab, so they're in no rush to leave."

"Guess the hotel gets paid as long as the credit card is open," I said. "How do you feel about crashing their party?"

The same desk clerk who had been so unhelpful the first time my family and I had visited the White Envelope stood behind the desk, her gaze sweeping the lobby like she was on a personal mission to keep out all intruders. That didn't seem like such a difficult job when the place was nearly deserted.

Sheriff Potts strode up to the desk while I hung back, suddenly interested in a piece of artwork that hung on the opposite wall. She flashed her badge and said, "I need the room numbers for Charles Reed's crew members."

"Do you have a warrant?" the desk clerk asked, apparently unswayed by the sheriff's uniform and commanding presence. "Here at the White Envelope, the privacy of our guests is top priority."

"It doesn't bother you that the man who has paid for their rooms is dead?"

The desk clerk seemed unruffled, even flashing a hospitable smile toward the sheriff. "The rooms were paid for in advance through tomorrow, when the festival was scheduled to end."

The tension between the two women was palpable, and I resigned myself to the fact that it didn't look like we'd be able to speak to the crew members, unless the sheriff was able to procure a warrant before the crew members left the following day.

But then I saw a man in swimming shorts and a towel slung over his shoulder exit the elevators to our right and walk toward the outdoor pool. His arms were large and muscular—exactly as a hot air balloon crew member's would be.

I left Sheriff Potts to her staring contest and slipped across the lobby, catching up with the man as he exited through the glass doors that led outside.

"Excuse me, are you one of Charles's crew members?" I asked, shielding my eyes against the bright sun.

The man turned, startled. "I didn't know anyone was left in the hotel. The place pretty much cleared out yesterday. You a cop?" His gaze took me in, making me uncomfortable. "Nope, definitely not a cop. Not with that figure."

Even though I was wearing jeans and a T-shirt, I felt like I needed to cover up even more.

"Um...no. Not a cop. I was hoping to express my condolences to Charles's crew members. Were you on his team?"

The man's posture relaxed, and he sauntered over to

the pool, almost like he was showing off. Like he expected that if he flexed his muscles enough, I'd have no choice but to throw myself at him. Never mind that the man had to be at least fifteen years my junior.

He tossed his towel and flip flops on a nearby pool chair, then dived into the water, his form perfect. It wasn't until he'd reemerged, dripping, that he bothered to answer the question.

"Yeah, I was on his team. But I doubt any of us need your condolences. We were here for the money and the nice hotel room. Doesn't look like we're likely to be paid, so we're taking advantage of the amenities and stocked fridge while we can."

I smiled and laughed, like this was the funniest thing I had ever heard. That was what women did to keep men talking, right? Make them think we were hanging on their every word. It had been a while for me, and I was a bit rusty in the men department, but it seemed to work.

With a too-large smile, I extended my hand toward him. "I'm Maddie."

He took my hand, his still wet, and held on a beat too long. "Cliff."

Once I managed to extract my hand, I sat at the pool's edge and removed my shoes, rolling up my pant legs. "Cliff, just how many people did Charles have on his team? Seems like he treated you well."

Cliff snorted. "He had too many, and frankly, the room upstairs was getting a bit crowded. That's why I came down here for a swim. Too much testosterone." His gaze settled on me again as I dangled my legs in the water.

My first inclination was to pull back, but I forced myself to stay. This was our only chance to find out what the crew actually knew.

"Still, being a crew member for someone the caliber of Charles Reed must have been exciting."

Cliff swam toward the opposite side of the pool with smooth strokes, then back again, once again showing off his muscles. His abs were just as ripped as the rest of him, and he grabbed hold of the side where I sat, smiling up at me.

It made my skin crawl, and it took focusing on a spot just beyond his head to help me hold his gaze.

"Exciting?" he said. "There were six of us, and we all knew that we were just there for show. Half the time, we were playing cards just to pass the time. Sure, we helped set up the balloon, and it took a couple guys to chase it down. We took turns for that. But most of the time, we felt as if we were wasting away. As far as Charles's caliber, he was in short supply of that."

"Oh." I feigned disappointment. "I've heard we're not supposed to meet our celebrity idols—that they'll only let us down. Still, I can't imagine anyone wanting him dead. I heard that his pilot pushed him over the edge of the basket. It's awful, is what it is."

"No, it was a favor to the rest of humanity. There was a crew member, not one of ours, thank goodness, whose wife left him for Charles. A week later, Charles dumped her for a younger blonde. Ruined their marriage and didn't even feel bad about it. Just said *sayonara*. And that's the tip of the iceberg. You ask me, it's a miracle someone didn't throw him overboard sooner."

I raised a hand to my mouth, my eyes wide in feigned shock. "What do you think he did to the pilot?"

Cliff raised a shoulder. "Who knows? The pilot was a last-minute add-on. Maybe he was planted by the bookie that Charles owed money to. Or maybe the pilot's wife was one of the casualties of Charles's love life."

"Weird that the balloon wasn't tethered, though, wasn't it? I was trying to get closer so I could get one of Charles's trading cards—I have four of them already, but I can always use another one—and saw it rising above the others. It was very disappointing."

Cliff hesitated, then pushed off from the side of the pool, eyeing me warily. "You sure seem to know a lot about what happened that night."

I put on an air of desperation. "Not nearly enough. Whatever your feelings about Charles, the man had a mystique about him, you know? An air of mystery."

"Yes, which is why he's dead. You want mysterious? A call came over the radio, asking us to untie the tethers as quickly as possible. We were told to cut them if we had to."

There was no need to act surprised at this announcement; I was genuinely taken aback. "Charles Reed asked you to untie the tethers?"

"He identified himself as Charles, but he sounded different. We knew not to question orders, though. That never went well. So one of the guys cut the tethers."

I pulled my legs out of the pool and let them drip off the edge. "And you didn't question the urgency?"

Cliff scowled. I was losing him. "You try working for the man, then you can judge me."

"I can't. He's dead."

I stood and unrolled my pant legs. They were a bit damp, but the information was worth the momentary discomfort. "Thanks for the chat, Cliff. I should get going."

He seemed surprised, like he'd thought I was there just for him. "Leaving already?"

"I have a murder to solve."

"B-but—"

I noticed security making the rounds and knew I'd need to hurry before they caught me wandering around the same place I'd been last time they'd kicked me out. Knowing my luck, that was exactly why they were here—looking for me.

"Sorry, but I'm not exactly supposed to be here. We'll have to catch up another time."

And then I walked the opposite way security had gone, except every door that led back into the hotel was locked, and I needed a room key to get back in. Out through the side gate it was.

By the time I reached the front of the hotel, Sheriff

Potts was waiting for me by her car. She noted my damp pant legs and smirked.

"Go for a swim?"

"Something like that. You get anything interesting, or did the desk clerk hold you off, still going on about needing a warrant?"

The sheriff's smile dipped. "I hate working with people like that—think they're important. Love the power that the law provides them."

"Oh, you mean she's a cop?"

As soon as I said it, I wished I could take it back. The sheriff and I had just started being on friendly terms, but the look she gave me now was not that of a friend.

"Most police officers do not choose the job for a power trip," she said, her gaze hard. "I've lost a friend—a partner —to the job. Because he was trying to keep people safe. Never minimize what it is that we do."

Duly noted.

"I'm sorry. You're right. Want to know what I got by flirting with a crew member?"

Sheriff Potts raised an eyebrow. "You flirted with a younger guy to get information?" She paused to appraise me. "I'm impressed—didn't think you had it in you."

I was unsure if I should be offended and decided to ignore the comment. "The crew member who ran around cutting the rope—he wasn't in on some scheme. An order came through the radio to untie the ropes as quickly as possible, and cut them if necessary."

"Charles Reed?"

"I don't think so. The poison had probably already done its damage. The crew member said it was supposed to be Charles Reed, but that he sounded different. Not quite like himself. But those guys, they were used to immediately following orders, no questions asked. So someone sprang into action and cut all the ropes."

Sheriff Potts seemed deep in thought as we slid into the car. "A man, then."

I gave a quick nod.

She released a long sigh. "Each crew is on their own radio frequency. Things are not looking good for your friend Andrew."

17

"What do you mean things aren't looking good for Andrew?" I stared at the sheriff as she drove me back to my motel.

Sheriff Potts glanced at me before her attention returned to the winding road. "Andy was up in the basket with Charles. He had access to all the food and wine and wasn't allowed to partake of any of it himself. A great excuse to why he hadn't eaten any of the poisoned food. He's strong enough to lift Charles over the edge of the basket, and he had a radio on him. He could have easily called in to the crew to cut the tethers. And let's not forget that he has motive. I'm sorry, but everything points to him doing it."

"But Andy said that Casey lifted Charles over the edge. She won weight-lifting competitions, and her family has a reputation to protect. And the fact that it was a man who called over the radio doesn't prove anything. It still could have been another crew member. They would have had access to the food before the balloon went up. Can't you call them into the police station or something? They have to be questioned."

The sheriff hesitated, then shook her head. "No. I'm done sticking my neck out for you. If this guy wasn't a friend of Ruby's, I would have already drawn up the paperwork and transferred him to a different facility so he can await indictment." She paused. "Maddie, I'm done. And I'm heading back to Amor to rethink my life choices."

Anger coursed through me. And desperation. There was no good answer. Sheriff Potts could be right. Maybe Andy really had done it. Maybe I had to call Ruby and tell her that I was sorry, but Parker was going to need to find another crewmate, because this one was guilty of murdering someone.

"Stop the car," I said.

Sheriff Potts' gaze whipped toward me, surprise etched in her features. "Sorry?"

"Stop the car," I repeated, more forcefully this time. "I need some air. Time to think. I'm not going to get it at the motel, and I'm certainly not going to get it here in this stuffy car."

The sides felt like they were closing in. I needed room to breathe.

"But we're on a deserted stretch of road," the sheriff said, seemingly trying to stall for enough time to get me back to the motel. "There isn't any cell service here, and you wouldn't be able to contact anyone. I'm not going to abandon you here."

"It can't be that long a walk," I said, my breaths coming faster. "But I'm tired of this. Tired of figuring out who hated who enough to kill them. Tired of thinking someone is a good, kind person who was innocent of any wrongdoing, then questioning everything I've believed."

The sheriff was quiet for a moment, but she didn't make any move to stop the car. "That's what makes you such a good psychologist," she finally said. "You see the good in people. There can be facts staring you in the face, and you still choose to ignore them and see the essence of who a person is. You don't judge them. You help them, and you do a lot of good. The town of Amor needs you. And frankly, the police department is better off because of you. Because you see the good in people, but you also care about the truth and not jumping to conclusions. You're not afraid to face the facts, but you want to be absolutely sure of them before you do anything rash."

I sensed a "but" coming. And it did.

"But we don't have the luxury of months or years of therapy sessions to get to the essence of our suspects. We have until the end of today. While you were questioning that crew member, I received a phone call. The police chief is happy with my service while I've been here, but they feel that with the groundwork I've done, they can take it from here."

"Meaning you did the hard work, and now they're happy to take credit for the arrest and get the festival back in good standing."

Sheriff Potts nodded. "Pretty much." She paused and glanced at me. "I've asked them to give me until the end of the day."

My breath whooshed out. The sheriff really did have my back or was at least trying to. End of the day, though. That wasn't long. And I wasn't sure my kids would appreciate me being gone even longer than I had been.

My kids.

"I think it's best I go back to the motel," I said.

The sheriff nodded and gave the gas pedal a little more pressure. She never said *I told you so*, and I appreciated that.

I FACED MY KIDS, much like a drill sergeant, pacing in front of them, attempting to gather my thoughts. "Okay, troops. We have less than eight hours to solve a murder. We've been through this before, and we can do it again."

A knock on the door.

I looked to Flash and Lilly, but they gave me blank looks, like they weren't expecting anyone.

When I opened the door, Benji stood on the other side.

"Mind if I come in?" He was looking around, anxious, almost like he thought he'd been followed.

I quickly ushered him in, and his eyebrows popped up when he saw the kids sitting cross-legged on the bed, waiting quietly for the meeting to proceed.

"Am I interrupting something?" he asked, glancing back toward the door, as if wondering if he should leave.

"Just a tactical planning session," I said, as if this was something we did every day. "Why do you look spooked, though?"

Benji threw on a smile, but it felt like it was for the benefit of the kids. Like something was bothering him and he was unsure if he should talk about it in front of them.

"What you need to say can be said in front of the troops," I said, resuming my drill sergeant pose, legs spread and my hands clasped behind my back.

Benji hesitated. "O-kay." He gave one more anxious glance toward the kids before saying, "I think someone's watching your motel room."

Aw, crap.

I moved to look out the window, but Benji grabbed my hand and pulled me back. His touch felt natural, and I didn't drop his hand right away, but then I saw Lilly's raised eyebrow and I crossed my arms. When Benji and I had been younger, we wouldn't have thought anything of it. We'd been comfortable with each other.

Kids changed things, though. They read more meaning into things than they should, and judging by Benji's conflicted expression, I wondered if he was doing the same.

"You don't want them thinking you're onto them," Benji said. "I already called the sheriff. She's going to swing by and check things out. I figured it would look natural enough if I came up to your room, but we shouldn't leave until we get the all-clear from Potts."

Maybe I should have let Benji speak to me in private—I hoped we hadn't scared the kids.

On the contrary, they both seemed to be itching to move back the curtain, just as I had attempted.

"How many are out there?" I asked.

"Just one. Maybe no one," Benji said. "It was that desk clerk from downstairs."

Valerie. Why would she be watching the room? An uneasy feeling settled over me. In a rundown place like this, would they have set up security cameras? Were we being watched that morning when the sheriff came by to visit? And again when I left with her? Maybe the killer thought we were getting too close to the truth.

I shook my head, not wanting to get ahead of myself. "We're not going to think about that. We only have a few hours until this investigation is handed over to the local police, and we all know that that means Andy will be officially charged with the murder of Charles Reed. That's fine, if he actually did it. But that's what we need to find out." I turned to Flash. "Did you find anything new?"

He had his computer sitting next to him, and he picked

it up, his fingers racing across the keys. "I managed to pull up registration information for each of the balloons and their crew members. Most balloons only had two or three crew members, whereas Charles Reed had six. It would make it easier for crew members to slip away because they could take breaks more often, and no one would be checking up on them unless they didn't return for their turn to keep their eyes on things."

"Good work," I said, no longer caring that my son was accessing websites he certainly didn't have permission to. At least this one wasn't a government website.

I turned to Lilly. "Anything else you discovered in those pictures of the basket?"

She picked up her camera and flipped through a few pictures, her lips downturned, almost like if she looked again, something might pop out at her. Never mind that she'd already been studying them for two days now. "Nothing new," she said with a disappointed sigh. "Just a picnic basket full of uneaten food and five empty wine bottles. We already know there was no way that Charles Reed could have drunk all that and not died of alcohol poisoning. Nothing else stands out."

Alcohol poisoning.

"Flash, what was his blood alcohol level?"

Flash jumped back on his computer, presumably to the government website that I absolutely didn't approve of him being on. Except for extenuating circumstances.

"Point eleven percent."

That was way lower than I was expecting. Couldn't drive with that level, but hanging out in a hot air balloon? He'd be fine. He had certainly been drunk, but he hadn't been the pilot. And that wasn't two bottles of wine worth, like Andy had told me.

So, where had all that wine ended up?

18

It was mid-afternoon when my mom finally returned from her breakfast date. I'd been getting worried and had been tempted to go out and find her. I was sure that Arnold was a nice enough guy, from what I'd seen, but still, I'd neglected my mom long enough, I figured it was my turn to worry.

"Where have you been?" I asked her as soon as she walked in.

She gave me an amused smile. "Miss me?"

I gave her my best mom look. "I expected you home hours ago. If you're going to stay out, you need to at least send me a text."

My mom was laughing, and I tried to stay stern, but I couldn't help but laugh with her. My mom and I had exchanged roles. Except, as a teenager, I'd had the excuse of not owning a cell phone. My mom didn't have that luxury.

"What I meant to say," I said, "is how was it? Have a good time?"

I wasn't even sure why my mom had agreed to the date in the first place. She'd been spooked when she'd realized that Arnold and his sons were staying just a few doors down from us—wanted to keep this to casual flirting, and that kind of thing.

But then Arnold had knocked on our door the previous evening and asked my mom out for breakfast. She'd said yes so fast, the entire interaction couldn't have taken more than a few seconds, and then he had been gone.

She'd said that she felt bad for the man—that he was lonely since his wife had died—and that it was the respectable thing to do.

Never mind that she hadn't been able to stop smiling the entire time, and that she was grinning even wider now.

"Breakfast was good," she said, turning and pretending to busy herself tidying up our room, though it didn't need it. "Surprising to find a good *huevos rancheros* in this kind of place."

"Uh-huh. And how was the company?"

My mom's actions paused for a moment before she resumed straightening the one and only chair at the small desk. "It's refreshing to meet someone who is so easy to talk to. I didn't have to do all the work for once, which was a nice change." She threw me a meaningful glance.

Never mind that I had never asked her to carry a

conversation and instead had the opposite problem—getting her to stop talking long enough for me to get a word in.

"So, red or green?" I asked.

My mom raised an eyebrow. "What kind of question is that?"

I raised an eyebrow too. "In my experience, you don't truly know someone until you've discovered the little things. Sure, it's always good to know how many kids they have and if they have a criminal record or not. But that doesn't truly tell you about what kind of person they are. Lots of people have kids, and lots of people have never been in prison." I fought back a smile at my mom's stunned expression. "So, which is it. Red or green?"

My mom hesitated, and I stepped back in mock horror.

"Please tell me he didn't order his meal with red chile sauce."

"It gets worse," she whispered, her cheeks darkening. "He'd ordered before me, and I was so flustered, I told the waitress to bring me the same. It wasn't until she had walked away that I realized what I'd done."

I sank onto the bed. "Mom, we're a green chile kind of family. We never make exceptions."

"I know, I know." My mom sat on the bed next to me, and it dipped under her weight. "But it's his only flaw, I swear. Arnold is a complete gentleman. He opened doors for me, pulled out my chair, and showed genuine interest in me and our family. He even had the decency to act embarrassed when I asked questions about *him*. Most men just prattle on about their own accomplishments, strutting around like the peacock they presume they are. Not Arnold, though."

I nodded, feeling guilty that I'd ever felt unsure about the prospect of my mom dating again. She'd been alone too long—she needed this.

"Did you exchange phone numbers? Think you'll end up going with him on his national parks excursion after all?" I asked.

"I don't think so," my mom said, her words halting and unsure. "I thought he might ask me again, but he seems to have been consumed by this murder business. The poor man said he's not sleeping well, tossing and turning. He wondered if I had any information on who could have done such a thing. Unfortunately, other than knowing about the poisoning and us hoping that friend of Ruby's wasn't responsible for such a heinous thing, I didn't have much to tell him. He just wants to leave, you know. Doesn't even care about the festival anymore. Might not even come back to the next one, he said. Too many bad memories, and there are plenty of other locations he can choose from. Arnold was told they can leave tomorrow, though, so that's something. Must mean the police have what they need from the pilots and their crews."

More like they thought they did, and they were eager to close the case.

"Would you have gone if he'd asked?"

My mom stood, her knee looking like it was back to its old habits. Apparently, her knee had become something of a mood ring, and Arnold had done more good than my mom had realized. But now that he was heading out, leaving disappointment in his wake, my mom's knee was letting her know that it wasn't happy with this turn of events.

"You know, I think I would have."

As much as I was unsure about my mom dating again, I knew it made her happy, and the pickings weren't great in our little town of Amor. I couldn't just stand by and watch my mom walk away from the first man I'd ever seen make her smile.

Whether she and Arnold admitted it or not, they needed me. And who was I to walk away from someone who clearly needed my intervention?

I cringed, realizing that I had become my mother.

I NEVER HAD the chance to march over to Arnold's room and demand that he whisk my mother away to Zion National Park and wherever else was on his national park itinerary. As soon as I'd emerged from my room, Valerie showed up.

"You sure you don't want to spend a few more nights and take in the view?" she asked.

I looked at the nearly empty parking lot. "I'm sorry you lost most of your guests, Valerie, but I don't think there is anything else we need to stay for. The festival is done for the year, and we'll be heading back first thing in the morning."

"The thing is," she said, lowering her voice, "I came to warn you. You've immersed yourselves in Chuck's murder, and that wasn't a smart thing to do."

I tried to decipher the expression on her face, but I couldn't tell if she was concerned, scared, or warning me away for more sinister reasons.

"Why is that? The police asked for my help—I'm a psychologist—and I wasn't about to say no."

That was stretching the truth a bit, but since I had inserted myself into the investigation, Sheriff Potts had asked for help on an occasion or two.

Valerie released a long sigh and rubbed her eyebrow. "Because there are some people who don't want this murder to be solved. Not because they did the deed, mind you, but because they don't think the person should be punished. They feel like it was a gift to the community, of sorts, and they don't want to know if it was one of us or someone from out of town. They just want the police to stop sniffing around and let bygones be bygones."

I wondered if this had anything to do with the receptionist at that other hotel. She seemed like she'd be the type to tattle on us.

"I see," I said, folding my arms across my chest, like her words didn't affect me—like they didn't make me want to pack up the car right then and leave town. "The only problem with that is there is an innocent man currently sitting behind bars at your police station, and people think he did it. You wouldn't want an innocent man to be punished for something he didn't do, would you?"

Valerie hesitated, her cigarette half-falling from her lips. Maybe she would be okay with that, if she were protecting someone. Sacrificing a stranger for a loved one didn't feel too bad—until someone called you on it.

"Valerie, we're leaving tomorrow morning no matter what, but I'd feel a lot better knowing I'd done my best to help someone who was in desperate need of it. If you have any information on who might have killed Charles Reed, please, tell me."

I hated the pleading tone in my voice, but time was short, and I was running out of options.

"I'm sorry," she finally said. "I don't think I can help you." And then she cast an anxious glance over her shoulder and hurried back down the stairs to her office.

When I turned to see what Valerie had looked at, I saw Jeremiah standing in the doorway of his motel room. He was leaning against the doorframe, shirt off, and giving me an easy smile. I tried to keep my gaze on his face and not on his abs. All six of them.

"She bothering you about staying a few days longer?" he asked. "I don't know if you heard, but the pilots and their crews are free to go, and we're heading out first thing in the morning."

"As are we," I said.

"Of course, I'd be willing to stay a little longer, if I had reason." Jeremiah pushed off the doorframe of his room and walked toward me.

I had been about to ask if his father wanted company on his national parks road trip—put in a plug for my mother—but the scent of Jeremiah's cologne washed over me, and I knew I had to get out of there before I found myself in a situation that I simultaneously wanted and was terrified of.

"Well, I hope you find your reason, but I better get back to the kids and make sure they're doing okay. Good seeing you," I said, and I took a step back.

"Let me take you out for a goodbye dinner," he said, mirroring my movement and stepping forward. "To make up for last night."

"Last night?" My mind flashed to visiting Andy at the police station.

"You want me to tell you that it hurt when another guy came along, asked you out after I had, and you chose him? Fine, I will. It hurt. At least give me a fighting chance."

I could admit that going out to dinner with Benji might have come across as rude, but technically, Jeremiah hadn't asked me out. Only hinted at it.

I could have leaned into that hint and still gone out with him. So, why hadn't I?

I didn't need to answer that question because Benji showed up at that moment. He was driving too fast and skidded to a stop in the dirt parking lot. When he jumped out of the car, he looked panicked, but when his gaze landed on me, it held a bit of relief. Of course, then he saw Jeremiah, shirtless, and his lips turned down. His gaze jumped from me to Jeremiah and back again, as if he were trying to determine the situation.

As for me, I felt nothing but relief.

"Benji," I said, my smile too wide, but not caring. I hurried down the stairs toward him, leaving Jeremiah to watch.

"Maddie," he said, his voice low and almost guttural. "We need to check out of the motel now."

"But I still have until the end of the day to prove Andy's innocent."

He shook his head. "It's too late for that, and they plan on coming for you next."

19

I pulled back. "I don't understand. Valerie was just trying to get me to stay a few days longer."

"Yeah, I don't doubt that she was. The sheriff asked me to pass along a message. She wants you to know that she tried her best, but she's done. The police took over the investigation earlier than expected, and they are closing this as quickly as the paperwork can get done. They've also received reports of harassment against you, and are claiming you impeded a police investigation. They are talking about coming over here before you can skip town. They think you were working with Andy."

"B-but...how could they think that? I'd never even met the guy until we visited him at the jail. Not to mention the fact that we weren't anywhere near that balloon."

Benji gave a slow nod. "No, but your kids were."

Images of them climbing in the balloon and taking

pictures came to mind. I prayed the police didn't know about Flash's less-than-legal internet activities.

"All right," I said, "I'll get the kids. You don't think they'll pursue this further after we've left?"

"It didn't sound like it. These guys—they seem to like things easy and wrapped in a red bow. Booking you would look good, but they don't seem to want to go to a lot of effort for it."

This wasn't good. A bunch of backwoods police officers who were bored and thought they'd try fishing with a shotgun and see what they got. But they couldn't catch what they couldn't see.

Unless they got lucky, which was probably what they were counting on.

"Benji—" I started. There were so many things I wanted to tell him. He hadn't needed to hang around here after the murder, but he had, and I knew it hadn't been for the sightseeing. I realized now why I had jumped at the chance to go out to dinner with Benji, and not Jeremiah.

Because Benji made me feel safe. Like nothing bad could happen if I was with him. He made me laugh, and he loved my kids. He probably knew me better than anyone else in the world, including my ex-husband. He'd admitted that he'd loved me once—when we were kids. I found myself wondering if he could love me again.

I shook the thought away when I realized that Jeremiah was still standing on the balcony, leaning against the railing and watching us.

Benji was the best friend I could always count on, and that was all that mattered at the moment. He'd rushed over to get us checked out of the motel, and that was what I intended to do.

"I'll stop by the office," I told Benji. "Would you mind telling my mom and the kids to pack up?"

"Of course."

I paused, then gave him a quick hug. "And thank you." Then I hurried over to the office, pretending that Benji's touch hadn't ignited a longing that I'd never before felt with him. Longing for something that seemed just out of reach.

"Valerie?" I called, walking into the office. "You here?"

No answer.

"Valerie?" I said again.

There was still no answer, but after a long pause, there was a sneeze. She was there, but she didn't want me to know it. Maybe the police had gotten to her—told her to keep us occupied. It looked like we'd need to leave quietly.

"Guess I'll need to wait on the ice machine," I said loudly, then quickly left.

I assumed it was the other hotel desk clerk that had accused me of harassment, but what didn't make sense was the impeding investigation part. Sheriff Potts wouldn't have ratted me out, considering we'd been working together. And if they knew about the pictures from the day of the murder, why wait until now to bring it up?

None of this made sense.

Unless they had received an anonymous tip of some sort—some do-gooder who had seen things and claimed to be too scared to report it earlier.

Someone who thought we were getting too close and wanted to see Andy stay in jail, in order for them to remain outside it.

As soon as I reached our motel room, I burst in, ready to start giving orders so we could get out of there as quickly as possible, but came to a screeching halt when I saw my mom sitting on the edge of the bed, Arnold's arm around her shoulders. She looked like she'd been crying, and he was comforting her.

"Uh...sorry, I'll give you a minute. But Mom, I'd like to talk to you. Soon."

I then backed out and moved to the kids' room. As soon as I walked in, Lilly rushed forward and threw her arms around me. "Mom, what's going on? Benji said that we needed to erase anything incriminating off my camera and Flash's computer, then told us to pack up as quickly as we're able."

"I'm sorry, but it looks like our vacation is going to be cut short," I said, wondering about my parenting skills, considering the mess I'd gotten us into. I should have kept my distance from the murder, but I couldn't help myself. Once again, I'd put the needs of others ahead of the needs of my own family, and now we were literally running from the law. "Someone has been feeding anonymous tips to the police. They've taken back the investigation, showed

Sheriff Potts the door, and they intend on arresting me for harassment and impeding an investigation."

"They can't do that," Flash yelped. "You've done nothing wrong."

And I apparently needed to review with my children what was considered legal and what was...not.

"I walked a fine line," I said. "I thought I was doing what was best. But instead of giving you guys the vacation you deserved, I ran around town looking for a murderer. And look where that's gotten us."

"It got us a mother who was trying to prove a man's innocence. That's the kind of example we need," Lilly said. "Not someone who will turn their back because it will interfere with us having a good time. You've always cared about helping people, never wanting to say no, and that's the kind of mother we need."

Tears pricked at my eyes. I had the best kids in the world. Even if they did have a skewed sense of when to draw the line between helping someone and ending up in jail yourself.

I pulled them both into a hug. "Well, right now I don't want to test the local police on what they can and can't do. So, how about we finish packing up, eh?"

A knock on the door.

It was my mom, and even though she looked a bit worse for wear, she was standing tall, suitcase in hand. "Benji told me what's going on. I didn't pack your things," she said. "Can't go doing all the work, or you won't ever learn to do it yourself." As if I too were a teenager still living at home, needing to learn my life lessons.

But I thought I saw past what she was saying to what she meant.

That she was hurting, and she'd only had the energy to do the bare minimum. I was happy to pick up whatever slack was left.

"You okay?" I asked.

My mom glared, like how dare I call attention to the fact that she'd been crying and might be in need of someone to talk to?

"I'm fine. I only met the man a few days ago, and he was a fling, remember? Someone to pass the time with. And now that time has been spent, and we are leaving. It's as simple as that."

Then she busied herself with ordering the kids around, reprimanding them for throwing their items into their bags rather than folding them neatly, then proceeding to teach them the correct way to do it.

I threw a sad smile in her direction, then returned to my room for my own belongings.

"You about ready?" Benji asked, poking his head in. "Just heard from Sheriff Potts. She's been sticking around the station, much to their annoyance, to make sure that you get out of town okay before they do anything crazy. Sounds like they got a call that informed them of your intention to skip town. They're preparing to come out here now."

"They have all of my contact information, Benji." I gave a resigned sigh and threw the pair of shorts I currently held back down onto the bed. "It doesn't matter. They can find me in Amor, and I won't be in any better position than the one I'm in now. They want some kind of trophy out of this—accolades. And they're going to get it. The harassment charge is bogus, of course, but we could be accused of planting evidence, or removing it. My kids were in that basket. There had to be dozens of witnesses that could attest to it, and as their mother, all fingers will point to me. Especially because I've been working so hard to prove Andy's innocence. This doesn't look good, but it will look even worse if I leave."

Benji seemed surprised at my defeatist tone, and I had to admit that it was a new low for me. But what else was there to do? We'd tried to find someone else who could have poisoned Charles's wine. I wasn't allowed anywhere near the girlfriend or that hotel, no one knew who had prepared the food, everyone thinking that someone else had done it, and Andy couldn't prove he had nothing to do with it.

Benji pulled me into a tight hug and held me, as if his life depended on it. Or maybe more accurately, like *my* life depended on it.

"It's going to be okay," he murmured into my ear. "But we're going to leave this motel and not give them the chance to do this on their turf, okay? If they want to chase

you down to Amor, so be it. But then you'll have Sheriff
Potts protecting you. She can't do that here."

I held on for another moment, needing the extra bit of
courage, then pulled back and wiped at a stray tear.

"All right. Let's get out of here. Valerie was hiding in the
back of the office, pretending she wasn't there, so I'll just
leave the keys on the desk."

Benji helped throw the last few stray items into my bag,
then slung it over his shoulder. I took his free hand and
turned my back on the worst motel I'd ever stayed in, and
resolved to go somewhere to see the hot air balloons next
year. Somewhere murder-free.

I owed my kids that much.

20

If I had to hear another word about how amazing Arnold was, I was going to pull the car over and call a taxi. Never mind that we were in the middle of nowhere with no cell reception, let alone any other cars.

But it had been a full hour with no police sirens chasing us, so that was something.

"He really was a lovely man, wasn't he?" my mom said, her gaze following the desert landscape through her window. "Had a great sense of humor too. He had to, considering his balloon was a giant bucket of chicken. Just my luck. I had to meet the perfect guy, and then run away."

I tried to be empathetic—and I had been for the first forty-five miles or so—but then my mom had circled back to the beginning and started all over again.

"There are more lovely men out there if you give them a chance," I told her. "Now that you've allowed your attention to be snagged by one, there's no telling how many you'll find."

My mom released a dramatic sigh. "Yes, but there will only be one Arnold. I doubt I'd find another who flew his own hot air balloon. Or who had two doting sons. They are a strong family, and that's something that's important to me. Family. Arnold said they've been especially close the past couple of years since his wife died. The boys cooked and cleaned and took care of him for the first few months, allowing him time to grieve. And then there was Jeremiah's divorce, of course. It was Arnold's turn to return the favor and rally around his firstborn. Tragedy can do that for people, you know. It's what brought you back to me."

Yes, it had. And it made me feel guilty that it had taken my own divorce for me to begin the process of repairing my relationship with my mom. Funny that Jeremiah had never seemed like the divorced type to me, but then again, the only time we'd truly spoken was when he'd been hitting on me, and maybe that was exactly how divorced men responded to their newfound freedom.

"The other son, I never had a chance to meet him," my mom continued. "Great family, though. If I were younger, we'd have had beautiful babies."

"Grandma!" Lilly said from the back seat as Flash groaned. I'd nearly forgotten they were there.

I tried to push the thought out of my mind. "Arnold was happily married up until just a couple of years ago, remember?"

She waved her hand through the air, like it was inconsequential. "Yes, I know. I'm just saying. That there was a beautiful man. Said he couldn't ask me to travel with him, though. Said he'd brought up the idea with his boys, and they didn't seem to think it was a good idea. I don't know why Arnold traveling on his own is any better, but it was devastating to hear that his boys didn't think I'd be a good fit for their father. Kind of took the fight out of me, you know? I don't want to be where I'm not wanted."

"Maybe it's just that it's a big commitment to go cross country with a woman you just met—they were being protective. It doesn't mean they didn't like you."

"Yes, I suppose. And it's no wonder the boys are cautious, with the women of their lives leaving them right and left—no need for a new mama."

Women leaving them.

A vague memory came to mind, a thought clicking into place and then—

"We have to go back."

I took the first exit I came to, turned around, then jumped back onto the freeway going in the opposite direction.

My mom clung to the door, her expression uneasy. "Anything you want to share with the class?"

"Only that I'm pretty sure I know who actually killed Charles Reed, and why."

"Oh, is that all? Well, in that case, maybe you should

call Sheriff Potts and have her handle it. No sense in adding several hours to our trip."

That wasn't like my mom at all, and I shot her a questioning glance. "Are you afraid of running into Arnold again?"

"It would be awkward," she said, sitting up straighter—defiant. "After that tearful goodbye, and then I show back up again." She almost seemed disgusted with herself, like caring for someone was unbecoming.

I didn't know how to break it to her, but she was most definitely going to run into Arnold again. And she wasn't going to like the circumstances.

21

"This really isn't the best place for you to be," Sheriff Potts said, intercepting me as I walked across the hotel lobby. "The police chief is on his way, and the hotel has already made it clear how they feel about you being here."

"When Benji said the police wanted me for harassment and impeding the investigation, I also assumed he meant the desk clerk here. But she didn't even see me last time—her entire interaction was with you."

Sheriff Potts gave me a blank look. "Maddie, you're going to have to be a bit clearer if you want to keep my attention. It's dinnertime, I'm hungry, and I'm supposed to be heading back to Amor. The police chief decided he wanted to regain control earlier than had been previously discussed, and honestly, I was okay with that. We gave it an honest try, you and I. But in the end, we found nothing that could exonerate Andy. I'm sorry."

A call came through on my phone, and I held up a finger, indicating that I needed a minute. "Hey, Benji. I heard the police chief knows that we're here. How about the others?"

"Yup. Shared the good news with them."

When he didn't say anything further, I pressed him. "Well?"

"They jumped in their car before I'd even had the chance to leave. They should be getting there around the same time as the police chief, maybe a little earlier."

I sucked in a deep breath. "Thanks, Benji. Stay with the kids and my mom outside, will you? I don't trust them to not try to sneak in."

He laughed, but he knew it was true. "You got it, boss."

I hung up, then turned to the sheriff. "Mind stepping behind the desk, please? Just outside of view."

Sheriff Potts gave a dramatic eye roll. "Really, Maddie. I thought we were beyond this."

"I'm not going to ask if you trust me, because I don't want to know the answer. But will you do it anyway? Please?"

It was with some grumbling and trepidation, but Sheriff Potts moved behind the reception desk and through a door that stood partly open.

Speaking of reception, I wondered where the desk clerk had gotten to.

Didn't matter much when it was security who showed up instead. Wherever she was, she must have seen me coming and considered me dangerous. That likely had nothing to do with my limited interaction with her and everything to do with Casey.

"We're going to have to ask you to leave, Miss Swallows," one of them said. He seemed new—I didn't recognize him, anyway—and despite his gargantuan size, he didn't seem to relish what had been asked of him.

"It's *Ms. Swallows*," I said, taking a step backward. "But you might want to know that you are harboring a murderer here."

Another guard raised a skeptical eyebrow. "You are not allowed access to this hotel, or Charles Reed's crew members."

"But it isn't the crew members I have need to speak with, and they didn't file the harassment charge against me."

A loud crash sounded from the direction of the elevator, and then shouting. We all turned toward the disturbance, only to find Casey emerging with a hotel employee pushing a large cart with her luggage placed haphazardly on it.

"If I had wanted my luggage spilled all over the ground, I would have done it myself," she was saying, berating the poor employee, whose cheeks had darkened in embarrassment.

"Sorry, ma'am," he said.

Casey sauntered in front of the cart, her purse slung over one shoulder. I knew the moment she caught sight of me. Her steps faltered and her eyes narrowed.

"I thought I told you to keep me informed if that woman returned," she said, addressing the two security officers. "What is it that you are paid for, if you can't protect your guests from unwanted visitors?"

The security officers shared looks that seemed to say they'd been on the receiving end of Casey's rebukes before and they weren't sure what they had done wrong this time.

"We thought you were resting in your room and didn't want us to disturb you," the larger of the officers said, his words slow.

"You mean, you didn't want me to find out that you'd fumbled once again. Completely inept, both of you. Do a sweep of the hotel grounds. If I know this woman as well as I think I do, her children are snooping somewhere they shouldn't."

The two security officers shared nervous looks, like they weren't sure if they should follow orders from a guest. They didn't last more than a few seconds under Casey's glare before shuffling off to see if they could find my children. I hoped they'd stayed in the car with my mom like I'd asked.

Casey motioned with her head for the hotel employee to continue forward with her luggage, grabbing a chocolate as she swept past the reception counter. She hadn't taken more than a few steps, however, when the doors to the hotel burst open, and in strode none other than Jeremiah, Arnold, and a man who must have been the younger brother.

Followed by my mom.

"That's him," she yelled, pointing to Arnold's younger son. "He's the one who cut the tethers on the balloon."

Everyone froze where they were, each eyeing the others.

It was Casey who broke the silence.

"I don't know what kind of drama you have going on here, but I won't be a part of it." She moved to walk out the doors, but Jeremiah stepped forward, blocking her path.

"I don't believe our business with you is done. As soon as you heard that Andy had been released from jail, you knew they must have found new evidence," Jeremiah said, arms folded across his chest. "And you thought you'd check out early. But we can't allow you to do that, Miss McKinnon."

"My father—" she began to say, but Arnold cut her off.

"Your father is not here right now, and I'm fairly certain that he will deny knowing anything about what has gone on here over the past few days. You should have listened to him and never gotten yourself involved."

"You'd never have pulled it off without me." Casey tossed a glance toward me. "Who is she, your eyes and ears? Sent to keep tabs on me?"

"No," Arnold said, releasing a heavy sigh. Like he didn't like what he was about to do. "She's a nuisance."

My mom moved from where she'd been standing near the front doors, marched forward, and put her hands on her hips as she turned to face Arnold. "You don't get to speak that way about my Maddie. You said you liked her. That your wife had always wanted a daughter, and you could imagine having one just like Maddie."

Arnold took a threatening step toward my mom. "Don't you dare mention my wife."

My mom looked shocked at his change of demeanor and backed up until she stood next to me. "I don't understand. What happened?" she asked, her words broken.

"Arnold has been feeding information about our activities to the police, and others," I said. "I wasn't the one keeping tabs on Casey for him, he was the one keeping tabs for someone else. Casey's father, I'm assuming."

My mom's gaze moved from Arnold to Jeremiah, and then to the younger son. "I don't understand."

I felt so bad for her, being betrayed like she'd been. Arnold was the source behind all of the anonymous tips, because he'd gotten my mom to open up to him—to trust him. And this entire time, he'd been making sure we didn't know enough to cause damage.

"I don't understand, either," Casey said. "So, if you'll excuse me—"

"You're the brains behind the operation," I interrupted. "You knew the wine was poisoned and told Andy and Charles you were on a diet. But when we first visited you here at the hotel, you didn't think twice before grabbing a chocolate off the reception desk, like it was something you did each time you passed. You did it again, just a moment ago. That doesn't seem like someone who is on a strict diet."

Casey looked down at her hand and almost seemed surprised that the chocolate was there. Like it really had become habit—something she did without thinking.

"I might make an exception now and again," she said, attempting a graceful recovery.

But I had her nervous, and that was what I needed.

I continued.

"That night in the balloon, you didn't know which bottle of wine had the poison. Which meant that someone else had added it. When Charles didn't have a reaction to the first bottle, what did you do, accidentally spill it so he'd have to open another?"

Casey's lips formed a tight line. "You have no proof of anything."

"But you called out about how many stars there were that evening. Even as Charles lay dying, you were admiring their beauty. Which is funny, because with all the light pollution from a hundred glowing balloons, the stars were hardly visible at all. That was the cue for some-one...probably Jeremiah...to call over the radio, on the frequency you gave him, instructing the crew to cut the tethers."

Jeremiah raised an eyebrow and glanced at his father. "I thought you said she wouldn't be a problem."

"She's not," Casey snapped. "She still has no proof, and I certainly have no motive. Why would I need Charles dead?"

"I wondered about that. You don't seem to have anything against him. But then I thought about where Charles was getting his money—all of the rich and powerful people he'd befriended over the years. People like that don't just cut you in on their business deals when you're a nobody from a small town that no one has heard of. Which led me to a different conclusion. Blackmail. Just before coming here, I looked into your father's financial records. Seems like Charles Reed received payments quite regularly from your father. And I'm certain he's not the only one paying out."

I wasn't about to rat my son out, but it was really difficult not to brag. Flash was very good at what he did.

"H-how did you—?" Casey spluttered.

"And then there was Arnold and his family," I said, turning to where the three men looked positively murderous. "They aren't bad people."

My mom scoffed.

I shook my head. "No, I really don't think they are. They are sad. And angry. And they protect their family at all costs. I was told that Charles broke up many marriages, but one in particular stuck out to me. The ruined marriage of a crew member from a different balloon. And then my mom mentioned that Jeremiah had been divorced. I'll admit that it took some assumptions on my part, but the timing of the divorce was about right, and it made sense. Possibly Casey's father reached out to you, offered you money for your help, and you'd get your revenge."

For the first time since I'd met him, Jeremiah looked frail. Human. Like the slightest wind would break him. "He deserved everything he got," he said, choking on his words.

"Maybe. But Andy didn't. He didn't go along with the plan to make Charles's death look like an accident. He didn't accept money to stay quiet. You probably thought he had to, considering you were his brother-in-law. Yes, I know that your wife was his sister. Maybe you thought Andy should be as angry as you were. Maybe you thought that was why he agreed to be Charles's pilot. Because he was finally going to do something about it."

"The man never had a backbone, just like his sister," Jeremiah spat out. "And everything that's been said is going to stay in this room." His eyes flashed angrily, but before he could do anything, the police chief strode through the back of the hotel lobby.

"Someone was blocking the front door, and I had to come in through the side," he said, moving slowly. Valerie was by his side, flashing her yellowed teeth in a wide smile.

"Told you I would do good, honey," she said. "I know that you didn't want to know who done it, let bygones be bygones, but it's better this way. Look how guilty he looks. And now the arrest is yours, not the sheriff lady's."

I spluttered, "You're dating the police chief?"

"Married to him, actually," she said.

I'd obviously not figured out everything.

"But you don't know anything," I said. "You don't even know who you're arresting. This belongs to Sheriff Potts." And she'd finally get to leave Amor—get a better job that made her happy.

Sheriff Potts appeared from around the corner of the reception desk. "I'm not here fighting for jurisdiction, Chief. I just want justice placed where it's deserved. You can take the credit." She held up her phone. "I'll transfer the audio file to you."

"But Sheriff—" I started.

She held up a hand, stopping me. "It's fine. I don't need it. Charles Reed was a local, so they can handle the details."

And then she walked past me and out of the hotel.

The police chief looked quite pleased with himself, even though he hadn't done a thing and the evidence had literally just been handed to him.

"In case you're wondering, you're arresting everyone in this room except me," I said, "and you can release Andy. He's innocent."

Arnold's mouth dropped open in confusion as his gaze bounced between me and the police chief. "But I thought... he'd already been released. We ran into that friend of yours at the motel, and he told us that Andrew was on his way home."

"Yeah, that wasn't true." I lifted my hands as if to say, *what are you going to do?* then hurried out of the hotel to try to catch the sheriff before she left.

"Potts," I called after her.

Sheriff Potts didn't turn and glare like she usually did when I used only her last name. Instead, she paused for a brief moment, then continued walking, as if she hadn't heard me.

"You shouldn't have done that," I tried again. "Shouldn't have let that police chief get the credit for your work."

This time she did stop.

With a glance over her shoulder, she said, "It wouldn't have made a difference for me, and it was the right thing to do. I'll see you back home."

And then she continued on.

Home.

Looked like sometime in the past few days, Sheriff Potts had become one of us.

And yes, it was about time we returned home.

The hot air balloons would return, and when they did, we'd be there.

22

A blindfold covered my eyes, and I squinted against it, hoping to catch the slightest clue as to where I was being taken.

Nothing.

No matter how I moved my head, tilted it, or scrunched my nose, that blindfold wasn't going anywhere.

The only sounds were of the car speeding along a highway somewhere, and that wasn't much of a clue.

I admitted defeat and settled back into the seat.

The car slowed and turned onto what sounded like a rocky dirt road. As we drove, I could hear the pings of the pebbles shooting out from under the car's tires.

My lips pulled up into a smile, and I sat up straight as I yelled in triumph, "The ghost town. We're going to the ghost town we used to visit as kids."

I tore the blindfold off, confident in my answer.

Sure enough, the dilapidated buildings came into view. Memories rushed over me. And happiness. A lot of happiness.

"I told you we wouldn't be able to fool your mom," Benji told the kids in the back seat. "She won the extra slice of pie fair and square."

"Can we have extra for our efforts?" Flash asked. "I thought it was pretty ingenious of me to 'accidentally' let it slip that there have been fossils discovered out in the middle of this desert. She almost thought we were going to a quarry."

"And yet she still got it right," Benji said with a smile. "Next time, we'll get her."

"So...no extra dessert." Flash sounded so disappointed at the thought that I couldn't help but laugh.

"Extra dessert for everyone," I said.

Benji's mouth dropped open. "That's not how this game works, and you know it. There are no participation trophies. Either you win, or you don't."

He pulled the car to a stop next to a house that only had three walls, and we got out, stretching. The sun was just beginning to rise, so we had some time before we would set up the breakfast picnic we'd brought along.

I'd questioned Benji's choice of the early hour, but the colors that were now splashed across the sky made it all worth it.

"There aren't any rules about me sharing my extra dessert with everyone," I said. Because as a mom, that was what you did. Nothing was ever truly your own. But I was okay with that. These kids were my everything.

Besides, this brunch was to make up for spending Lilly's birthday rescuing a man from jail, not exactly top of the list for any teenage girl, and she deserved extra dessert. I hadn't found out until we came home that her friend had started dating the guy that Lilly liked, and they'd had a falling out, which was why she'd been more than happy to spend her birthday away from home, and away from those she'd thought were her friends. The new camera I bought her as a birthday present had helped ease some of the disappointment, but it couldn't heal all wounds.

I watched as Flash snuck the apple pie from the picnic basket and ran away with it, Benji chasing after him.

It didn't take long for Benji to come running back with the pie held high over his head, triumphant.

"Did you seriously just steal a pie from a kid?" I asked, teasing.

Benji skidded to a stop, his eyes widening in mock horror. "He started it."

"And I'm not a kid," Flash protested, running up, his breaths heavy.

"Perfect," I said, handing him a blanket. "That means you can help set up for breakfast. Make sure to put rocks down on the corners so they don't fly up like last time."

But then a loud noise from behind one of the buildings made us all turn. It was like the whooshing of air, combined with eerie haunted house type music—the stuff that nightmares are made of.

With the sun just barely making its presence known, the ghost town suddenly felt more eerie, and less beautiful, than it had a moment earlier.

"Murder investigations are one thing, but how do you feel about a ghost hunt?" Benji asked, looking nervous.

Lilly gave her head a vigorous shake. "Nope. I'm out. I'll eat breakfast at home, where there isn't a chance of being possessed by someone from the other side, thank you very much. For all we know, it could be Charles Reed coming back." She turned and walked briskly back to the car.

"I guess it's just the three of us," Benji said, glancing back at me. His eyes were uneasy, as the whooshing sounds continued.

I took a step back. "Do you remember the only haunted house I ever went to with you?"

Benji smiled and nodded. "You got so scared, you took the emergency exit."

"And I've never stepped foot in a haunted house since. Ghost towns are all fun and everything, but this one has never been haunted before."

Benji threw a glance at Flash. "At least you'll come with me, right?"

My teenage boy who was usually up for anything stepped back next to me. "Sorry, I'm with my mom and Lilly on this one. I don't care how beautiful that sunrise is, this is just freaky."

Benji's phone rang, and he pulled it out, glancing at it before answering. It was kind of early for someone to be calling.

"Yeah, I know," he said without the preamble of hello. "But they won't come. Cut the music, will ya?" He hung up and slid the phone back into his pocket.

"What's going on?" I asked slowly.

Benji no longer looked nervous but was instead grinning as the creepy music stopped, though there was still a whooshing of air. "Will you please come with me?"

That man was up to something, and I had a feeling it was the reason he'd insisted on pulling my family out of bed at six o'clock in the morning.

I nodded. "All right." The kids balked, but when Benji and I started toward the abandoned buildings without them, they must have decided they'd rather be scared with us than scared without us, and they hurried to catch up.

I walked up a set of rotten steps, but Benji motioned for me to follow him around the building rather than entering it.

"You notice the condemned warnings they've put up since we were last here?" Benji pointed out. "I'd rather you not join the ghosts."

Seemed fair.

Once we rounded the building, my breath caught.

A hot air balloon.

And not just any balloon. The genie lamp.

Charles Reed's balloon.

"He *is* back from the dead," Flash whispered.

As we drew closer, however, the man waving from inside the balloon was not the goateed man who had met a tragic end. Instead, a man who looked vaguely familiar stood in his place, though where I'd seen him before, I couldn't recall.

I knew the woman who stood next to him, though. And it wasn't Casey.

"Ruby," I called, hurrying forward. Which meant that the man with her must have been Parker.

She grinned and waved wildly as we approached the balloon. "Happy birthday, Lilly." Ruby turned to me. "We wanted to thank you and the kids for everything you did, and Benji said the kids hadn't gotten to see a balloon fly for all your time at the festival, and that Lilly had spent her birthday up there."

"But how did you end up with a dead man's balloon?" Flash asked.

I had the same question, though I'd have worded it a little differently.

"That would have something to do with me," Andy said. He stepped around from the backside of the balloon, where he and another man were holding it down. "Charles's family didn't want the balloon and said the police station could do whatever they wanted with it. And considering I, an innocent man, had been held in jail for several days, I figured it wouldn't be too much to ask."

I laughed. "And they just gave it to you?"

"They were happy to be rid of it." He turned to the other man, who was helping hold down the balloon. "I don't believe you've had the privilege of meeting Rafael. Managed to track the man down in Vegas and return his phone."

Rafael smiled and nodded in greeting. "Sounds like I missed out on an adventure."

Andy turned to his friend. "Is that what we're calling it now? Me nearly being convicted of murder?"

Rafael snorted. "You're out of jail, you're fine. Besides, you got a balloon out of it."

"A balloon that I promptly gave to Parker to replace his ruined one. I think you should at least take me out to dinner or something. Maybe a 'congratulations on not being a murderer' party."

Ruby cleared her throat. "How about the real reason we flew out this way, huh?"

Andy started, like he'd completely forgotten. "Oh, yeah." He turned to Flash and Lilly. "I understand that you never got to see the balloons fly. So, how would you like to actually go up in one?"

Both Lilly and Flash's jaws dropped, their eyes wide in shock as they turned to me. "Can we, Mom? Can we?"

I hesitated. Watching balloons fly was one thing, but being inside one was entirely different. "I believe the last time you flew, you crashed and these three had to rescue you," I told Parker, nodding toward Ruby, Andy, and Rafael.

His cheeks reddened. "Extenuating circumstances. It's the first time that's ever happened, and it will be the last."

"I don't know..."

The kids took that as a yes.

"I'm getting my camera," Lilly yelled, and ran back toward the car.

"I call shotgun," Flash said as he ran to get into the basket.

My stomach twisted, but I felt better knowing Ruby would be there. "There is no front seat in a hot air balloon," I called after Flash as he clambered inside.

"We'll have them back by lunch," Ruby said as Andy helped Lilly over the side of the basket.

Seeing the faces of my kids as they rose in the balloon, grins so big they took up half their faces, I was grateful for good people in the world. And that I was privileged to know them.

Speaking of good people...

I turned to Benji as Andy and Rafael jumped into their truck, ready to follow the balloon. "Thank you," I said. "For setting this up. It means the world to me. And to my kids. Seriously, thank you."

Benji looked down at the ground, as if embarrassed by my gratitude. "It was nothing. The subject of flying happened to come up when I was hanging out with Parker. Andy and Rafael were in town for a couple of days, and when I found out about Charles's balloon—well, it seemed only natural."

"Even so, thank you."

Benji's gaze lifted and met mine. It lasted for a moment longer than necessary, then he broke eye contact. "I guess that means it's just you and me left for this morning picnic of ours, huh?" He turned and started walking back toward the remnants of the ghost town. "I hadn't realized the kids would be going up in the balloon so quickly, and I packed enough food for the four of us."

"I'm sure we'll manage," I said, my stomach reminding me that it had been neglected for far too long.

Benji glanced back and smiled. "Yes, I think we will."

He took my hand as we walked, and I didn't pull away.

EPILOGUE

1 year later

"Two scones. Three chocolatey chocolate muffins—"

"You can just say chocolate muffin," Melinda said, glancing up from the pad of paper where she was taking down my order.

Yes, I could. But it was a chocolate muffin with chocolate chips and some kind of fudge swirl—it would be an insult to lump it in with every other chocolate muffin.

These ones were special.

"—five orders of your best biscuits and gravy. And five cups of orange juice. To go."

Melinda ripped off the piece of paper and stepped

back, handing it to the cook. She grabbed a prepared plate and walked around me, delivering it to a customer.

I was about to ask if she'd mind if I paid now—I was in a bit of a hurry. These were for Lilly's eighteenth birthday breakfast, after all, and the girl shouldn't be kept waiting. Not after the disaster of a birthday she'd had the year before. Before I had the chance, however, a plate shattered behind me, and Melinda hurried into the back for a broom.

From the look on her face, she wasn't someone I should be approaching for at least the next few decades.

And then a miracle happened.

Daniel, a man who had moved to town a couple of years earlier, appeared with a dustpan and convinced Melinda to let him help clean up.

I'd never seen anyone brave enough to approach Melinda like that.

"That's a brave man," someone said from behind me, echoing my thoughts. I turned to see Benji standing behind me in line. He must have appeared while I was watching the broken plate scene unfold.

I smiled at the sight of him.

"I know what you mean," I said. "She seems grumpier than usual."

Benji lowered his voice as we watched Melinda take a phone call in the back, the line at the counter growing longer.

"From what I hear, Melinda's upset about Bree getting

married," Benji said. "I heard she might not even go to the wedding."

Bree. Why was that name familiar?

My confusion must have been evident because Benji gave me an incredulous look. "Melinda's younger sister?" He paused, as if looking for a hint of recognition, but I had none. "I suppose it makes sense you don't remember her, considering she left for college and didn't return. Same as you."

I tried to ignore the guilty feeling the comment invoked. I didn't think Benji meant anything by it, but it still felt like just another person telling me that I'd betrayed the town—and the people in it—by pursuing my dreams. By chasing after something that Amor didn't provide. By forgetting everyone I'd left behind.

"Anyway," Benji continued, "she's getting married. It's out at White Sands National Park, though. Not sure if I want to make the trek."

Now I remembered where I'd seen the name—a wedding announcement had arrived at my mom's while I'd been visiting with the kids. Which my mom had promptly thrown in the trash. When I'd questioned her, she'd admitted that she'd never gotten along with Melinda and Bree's parents, that she'd turned down a job with them when I was young, and that this was their way of rubbing their successes in her face. Never mind that they'd moved from town a decade earlier, leaving Melinda in charge of the diner.

I doubted they ever gave my mom a second thought, and it was more likely they'd sent an announcement to everyone in town.

But Benji was saying he hadn't received just an announcement—but an invitation.

"What made you so lucky to be invited to the wedding?" I asked with a small laugh, unsure if I wanted to know the answer. What connected him to Melinda's family?

He lifted a shoulder. "My parents are friends with their parents. My mom and dad will be out of town, and they asked me to go in their stead."

Okay. That made sense. But jealousy raised its head at the thought of Melinda and Benji. The way she openly flirted with him, even when I was with him. It wasn't like we were dating, though. I often felt like we were moving in that direction, but the trajectory seemed to be two steps forward and one step back. Like something was standing in our way.

My thoughts were cut off when Benji said, "Why don't you go with me?"

"Sorry?"

Benji was nodding vigorously now. "Yes. That way I can appease everyone. I can make my appearance but also stave off any unwanted attention."

My hopes had risen for the briefest of seconds, but then dropped. I wouldn't be a date. I'd be a bodyguard.

"So...I'd be there as protection. An excuse."

"Yes. It's perfect!" Benji grinned, like he didn't see anything wrong with this.

And as much as I wanted to be annoyed at him for his cluelessness at how that might make me feel, I couldn't help but smile back.

Because Benji had just invited me to go away with him. To a wedding.

No meddling mother. No murders. Just us and White Sands National Park. A way for me to figure out my feelings for this man I'd known my entire life.

What could go wrong?

The End

ALSO BY KAT BELLEMORE

MADDIE SWALLOWS MYSTERY SERIES

Dead Before Dinner

Dead Upon Arrival

Dead Before I Do

BORROWING AMOR

Borrowing Amor

Borrowing Love

Borrowing a Fiancé

Borrowing a Billionaire

Borrowing Kisses

Borrowing Second Chances

STARLIGHT RIDGE

Diving into Love

Resisting Love

Starlight Love

Building on Love

Winning his Love

Returning to Love

ABOUT THE AUTHOR

Kat Bellemore is the author of both the Borrowing Amor small town romance series and the Maddie Swallows cozy mystery series. Deciding to have New Mexico as the setting for these series was an easy choice, considering its amazing sunsets, blue skies and tasty green chile. That, and she currently lives there with her husband and two cute kids. They hope to one day add a dog to the family, but for now, the native animals of the desert will have to do. Though, Kat wouldn't mind ridding the world of scorpions and centipedes. They're just mean.

You can visit Kat at www.kat-bellemore.com.